T0328754

flipped

If you want a break from hard news but still crave something close to headlines, this is a must-read. A kaleidoscope of intersecting lives and emotions, this book tilts you into a journey those grappling with the disappearances of loved ones are forced to navigate. From moms and teens to cops and crooks – and an array of individuals in between – these pages provide an intimate glimpse of the varying realities underpinning what happens when someone basically vanishes. The abrupt voids, the gnawing anxiety, the relentless cycles of questions … Hawthorne deftly delivers all this through the eyes of several characters, some of whom feel familiar. She takes us into their contrasting worlds, their homes and thoughts, and treats us to nuanced views. We dip into gritty organised crime, poorly resourced policing, small town quirks, and tenuous and tight relationships. *Flipped* first gently then firmly grips you, transporting you into other spaces and lives. While a work of fiction, given meticulous research and textured detail, this could easily be reality – a reality any one of us could suddenly find ourselves navigating.

– Caryn Dolley, author of *The Enforcers* and *To The Wolves.*

'Beautifully told against the backdrop of modern South Africa, with a cast of lovingly drawn, relatable characters, *Flipped* is a deeply moving tale and, at the same time, an unputdownable page turner.'

– Tony Park, bestselling author of *The Pride* and *Blood Trail.*

'*Flipped* begins with an irritation of teenagers and ratchets up through suspicion and time to nerve-racking suspense as a life ebbs away.'

– Jenny Hobbs, author of *Thoughts in a Makeshift Mortuary* and *True Blue Superglue*

'Hawthorne's darkly honest fiction trips us into believing one thing about this book before she turns the page into another – reeling all-too-human nightmares into intertwining stories about pain and love.'

– Janet Smith, veteran journalist and author

'I could not tear myself from these pages! A thrilling read with vivid imagery, which makes you question everything on a heart-racing hunt for the truth.'

– Quraisha Dawood, author of *Almost Me* and *Stirring the Pot*

flipped

Tracey Hawthorne

Published in 2023 by Modjaji Books
Cape Town, South Africa
© Tracey Hawthorne

www.modjajibooks.co.za

This is a work of fiction. All the characters, organisations and events portrayed in this novel are either products of the author's imagination or are used fictitiously.

ISBN 978-1-991240-04-0 (print)
ISBN 978-1-991240-05-7 (ebook)

Editor: Fiona Zerbst
Cover concept and artwork: Tanya Majo
Cover design: Santa van der Walt
Text design and layout: Liz Gowans

To the memory of
my mother Jessie Hawthorne
and
my friend Tracey Derrick

I

WINTER 2010

The river rose high inland. Hundreds of kilometres northeast of the ocean, up in the crags, as the winter rains began, its waters drew together. First as individual trickles, then as lively rivulets, they poured effortlessly past and over the shoulders of ancient rock formations, around scrubby trees clinging resolutely to the inhospitable flanks of the mountain, joining other streams. By the time they reached the plateau to begin their long journey to the sea, they had become one mighty waterway: the river.

Along its length it ran through the landscape, a life-giving artery irrigating crops, vineyards and orchards, filling reservoirs and supplying pumps.

The small town where Sergeant Tamara Cupido wielded her authority was about halfway along the river's length, and therefore also about halfway between its source and where it emptied out into the sea.

Several hundred years earlier, the river and its banks had been home to pods of hippos. Near the site of what was now the farm belonging to Charlie Chapel, the vast aquatic animals had once gathered in their dozens. Bulls, cows and calves submerged themselves in the cooling waters during the long, hot summer days. Perfectly adapted to their watery habitat, the enormous animals would slow-motion gallop with surprising grace along the river bottom. Pretty agile even on land, given their tank-like torsos and short, squat legs, they would climb the steep banks each night to graze for hours on short grasses, covering impressive distances in their steady search for food.

As more farms were pegged out, and towns established, the hippos' habitats were increasingly subsumed by human 'progress'. And where the needs of hippos and humans clashed, it was always people, with their guns, who won. The last hippo had been shot a hundred years before: it had, they said, attacked a farm labourer.

The river had always provided good fishing but the local species that had once swum in it had been supplanted by exotics. This wasn't a simple matter of one fish being much like another: the local populations had lived in long-term balance with the plants and other animals that called the river home; the exotic species, however, with their voracious appetites and breeding habits, played constant havoc with the river's ecology.

Here and there, alien plant infestations had also entirely replaced the indigenous trees that had previously exercised a benign control over the flow of the river, filtering its water and preventing erosion. These usurpers drank thirstily, soaking up runoff water. This reduced the river's flow, which in turn meant less water for agricultural and domestic use. Periodically along its length, chronic erosion had caused the banks to collapse and dump additional soil and sand into the water, and this had altered the natural architecture of the river bed, creating underwater hills and valleys that hadn't been there before.

In particularly wet seasons, like this record-breaking winter, the river's banks were unable to hold its massively increased volume. Upriver from the bridge that separated Sergeant Cupido's town from the farmlands to the east, the earth on either side of the racing waters had yielded to their colossal power. The river, violently alive, had surged up out of its bed, into vineyards and onto farmlands, spreading its fast-moving tentacles into orchards, submerging pump stations, turning dry depressions into ever-widening pools and footpaths into rivulets, then streams, then dams.

The bridge itself, a multi-arched concrete structure with a generous 200-metre length, and built high above the average water level, was more than adequate in normal circumstances. It had two lanes for vehicle traffic, and a hard shoulder on either side. The concrete crash barriers on the outer edge of the hard shoulders were about a metre high. Sometimes – when the weather wasn't so challenging – people pulled over and stopped on the hard shoulder. They leant over the barrier, watching the water flow by far below, and amusing themselves by throwing things into the river.

This winter, however, the floodwater crashing under the bridge had brought the water level very close to its underside. This terrifying deluge was also carrying debris, both organic and manmade – whole trees, branches and trunks, and litter and detritus of every kind imaginable, including large structures picked up and carried along as lightly as pieces of straw by the wild waters. This had accumulated on the upriver side, and it now looked as if beavers had built a dam there. This forced restriction of the river's passage around the bridge's arched supports concentrated the water flow and further raised its level.

The water roaring from the downriver side of the bridge, hurtling westwards towards the ocean, was deep, and it was moving at a rate of several hundred thousand litres a second.

1

At 2 a.m., Terry Bronson put on her boots, coat and scarf, and left her house, locking the front door behind her. She'd looked in on her friend, Nicky Hallett, who was dead to the world, snoring loudly. The little tabby cat, who'd claimed this room as her own since her son Patrick had left for varsity, was crouched uncomfortably, and clearly indignantly, at the foot of the bed.

Terry started her car, switching on the windscreen wipers and the demister for both front and back windows. Scratching around in her bag, she found her glasses, and put them on.

She hated driving in the dark, and it was infinitely worse in the rain – although, fortunately, it seemed to have stopped for now. She hoped it would hold off for a while.

She pulled away from the pavement and drove to the stop-street at the end of the block, then she turned left, right at the next stop, and left onto the main road to the farmlands.

This would have been the route her daughter's friend, Jess, had driven earlier – if, Terry thought, Rosanne and Jess had actually gone to a party on Ryan Chapel's family's farm, where they'd said they were going, and not somewhere else completely. Her 17-year-old daughter, Rosanne, or Annie, as most people called her, had become so economical with the truth that Terry never knew when she was being told fact or fiction; she suspected that almost everything Rosanne told her at the moment was a lie of some dimension.

At this time of night and in this weather, the road was deserted, for which Terry was grateful. She drove slowly, concentrating hard. It was pointless for her to scan the roadsides. Her extreme shortsightedness and night-blindness made it impossible for her to see much beyond the headlights. What she did do was open the car's front windows. If there was anything critically audible in the cold, still night, she didn't want to miss it.

She drove the eight kilometres towards the bridge like this, hearing the shushing sound of the car's wheels on the wet road, but nothing else. Twice she had to swerve to avoid tree branches lying in the road, and once a tiny creature, its eyes glittering in her headlights, dashed across in front of the car. Thankfully she was driving slowly enough for it to make the crossing unharmed.

Approaching the bridge, Terry could hear the roar of the water. The heavy rains had swollen the river to the point where it had broken its banks, flooding the surrounding vineyards and putting them under water that would take weeks to subside.

She drove slowly onto the bridge, and the sound of the river became much louder. It was the continuous thunder of an unstoppable life force ... sobering to think that mere water could make such a powerful noise. She had to swerve to avoid something low, squat and solid protruding a short distance from the hard shoulder into her lane, but, again, it wasn't hard to do because she was driving so slowly.

Terry exhaled with relief when the car got safely to the other side.

The Chapel farm was down a dirt road to the left, about a kilometre on. As far as she could tell, the only thing growing there was old cars in various states of dilapidation, up on bricks. The front yard was full of them.

She'd dropped Rosanne at the farm on a few occasions since her daughter had started seeing their son, Ryan. The father seemed to be as poorly socialised as his offspring. Although Rosanne had absolutely forbidden her mother to come in and meet him, Terry had waved to him from the car from time to time, but she never got a friendly reaction. Once there'd been a very brief, almost imperceptible nod, but usually it was just a short, hard stare. The mother, according to Rosanne, had run off when Ryan was a baby. No surprise there.

The dirt road was a horror story, churned to mud by the rain and the passage of other vehicles that had come this way before her. Terry tried to keep her speed slow and steady but she could feel the tyres slipping, and was afraid that if she stopped, she wouldn't be able to get the car moving again.

She hunched over the steering wheel, staring through the windscreen at the chocolate-coloured waves of road ahead, carefully navigating holes and ridges, the car occasionally slewing sideways. She was all too aware of the powerfully rushing water of the river in the inky darkness somewhere to her left, running parallel to the road. Fearful and anxious, she was suddenly also filled with anger at Rosanne: how dare she put her through this bloody worry!

At last, she saw the entrance to the Chapel farmstead on the right. It had no identification other than an untidy hand-lettered sign wired to the gate that read 'Trespasers will be shot. Survivors will be persecuted'. The message – and the mistakes – tell you all you need to know about the people living here, she thought uncharitably.

She stopped her car in front of the gate. Her headlights illuminated the car graveyard. She could vaguely make out the looming shape of the house behind it, and could see only one dim light on in a room at the far end of the building.

She turned off the engine, killed the lights and sat quietly, listening.

There was silence, other than the perpetual rumble of the invisible river, now behind her, across the muddy road. The party – if there had indeed been a party here – was clearly over.

She took her phone out of her coat pocket. It was 2.45 a.m.

There were no text messages, no missed calls, no voicemails.

She dialled both girls' phones again but, as she knew they would, both went straight to voicemail.

Now what? she thought to herself.

She could wake up the Chapels and find out if Rosanne and Jess had been here, and if so, when they'd left.

But had Rosanne been telling the truth?

'Aaarrgh!' The sound of her frustration was very loud in the still night. She rested her head on the steering wheel for a moment, trying to decide what to do.

Because she suddenly felt spooked sitting alone in the pitch dark, she switched on the car headlights again, and out of nowhere a huge dog – a boerboel – appeared, hurling itself into the pool of light at the gate, and barking furiously.

'Jesus,' Terry said to herself.

A second dog, equally massive-shouldered and lion-headed, joined it. The barking was frenzied and ear-splitting.

Terry saw one light, then another, go on in the house.

'Well, that answers the question of whether or not to wake them up,' she said to herself, as she got out of the car. She didn't want to get too near the dogs, so she walked to the front of the car and stood in the headlights, where she would be clearly seen.

Soon, she heard the front door opening and a voice calling, 'Boetie! Bliksem! *Shaddup!*'

'Hello,' Terry called.

She could see a male figure now, coming towards her, his right hand lifted to shield his eyes against the car headlights.

'Switch those bladdy lights off, man,' came a voice, shouting over the barking of the dogs.

'Sorry,' Terry muttered, quickly going back around to the driver's door, leaning in and switching the headlights off but leaving the parking lights on.

The man was trying to pull the dogs away from the gate and get them to be quiet but wasn't having much success. The ongoing noise was nerve-shattering.

'I'm looking for my daughter!' Terry shouted. It was clear that there wasn't going to be any chance of a conversation – best to get right to the point.

'So?' the man shouted back.

'She and a friend were at a party here earlier. She didn't come home.'

She wasn't sure how much the man was hearing over the dogs' barking, which seemed to be getting louder and more frenzied with each passing moment.

'*Wait!*' the man yelled, as he finally got hold of the dogs' collars and dragged them away from the gate.

Terry's eyes slowly began adapting to the darkness, and she could vaguely see the man pulling the struggling dogs to the left side of the house. She heard the metallic sound of a gate opening, then some scuffling, and finally the gate closing. The dogs continued barking but at least now the sound was somewhat muted by distance.

The man came back, panting slightly. He was shortish and fleshy, with short-cropped dark hair and an almost comically large, untidy moustache. He was wearing bright-red pyjama bottoms that were too long for him and trailing in the mud, and a long-sleeved winter vest that may once have been white. His familiar features – the short, vaguely pig-like nose with its large nostrils, the heavy-lidded eyes with their hint of both menace and stupidity – made it evident that he was Ryan's father.

'Sorry about this,' Terry said, going for a self-effacing tone that she hoped would elicit a sympathetic response. 'My daughter came to a party here earlier and she hasn't come home.'

'Who's your daughter?'

'Rosanne. Annie. Annie Bronson.'

Mr Chapel made an expression of distaste that indicated that not only did he know exactly who her daughter was, but also how little he thought of her. Terry felt like slapping him, but she needed to keep him on her side until she knew exactly where Rosanne was, and if she was safe.

'Ja, my son had some friends over,' the man conceded ungraciously. 'I know Annie. She wasn't here.'

Terry's heart sank. This was what she'd been afraid of. If Rosanne had lied to her about where she was going, and Jess wasn't around to provide the truth, how was she going to find her?

'Are you sure?' she asked. 'She said she was coming here.'

'Pfff.' The sound of scorn made by Chapel senior made it clear how little value he put on anything Rosanne said. 'I know your girl,' he repeated. 'I can tell you she wasn't here.'

'*Jesus*,' Terry said, her anger suddenly boiling over. 'My daughter is missing. Can't you be a little more helpful?'

'If you'd taught that little slut better manners, maybe you wouldn't be having to look for her in the middle of the night,' Chapel said.

Terry's mouth fell open. 'I can't believe an adult – a *parent* – would say something like that!' she exclaimed, aware of how prissy and powerless she sounded. But she was totally taken aback by his attitude. It was one thing to find teenagers unbearable – by and large, they were – but it was quite another to treat what may be a very serious situation with such callous dismissiveness.

The man turned and walked away, calling over his shoulder, 'I'm going to let the dogs out. You'd better get going.'

What the fuck does that mean? Terry thought. Surely he can't be threatening to set his dogs on me?

As unlikely as it may have seemed, she wasn't going to take any chances. She got back into the car and started the engine, put the headlights on full glare and revved the motor. It was partly a statement but also just to get rid of some of the frustration and anxiety she was feeling.

Chapel, his dumpy body now spotlit, continued walking towards the side gate, where Terry could see the enormous dogs throwing themselves against the wire. Casually, without turning, he lifted his right hand and gave her the middle finger.

'Just fucking unbelievable,' Terry muttered to herself, reversing into the muddy road.

It took all her self-control to pilot the car safely back along the dirt road. She desperately wanted to gun it, for various reasons: she wanted to put as much space between herself and that ghastly man as she could; she wanted to get home because there was a chance that she'd find the girls there; and she was feeling overwhelmed with worry and anger.

Finally reaching the end of the muddy road, and, turning right onto the tar, she closed the windows and turned up the heat. Gosh, it was cold.

The rain had started again, although it was only a light drizzle.

Once back over the bridge, she kept her speed at a steady fifty kilometres per hour, peering out into the night in the hope of catching sight of ... what?

2

'You're not going out dressed like that, young lady.'

Terry could hardly believe these words had come out of her mouth but, good god, the state of her child defied belief – she was dressed in next to nothing, but where she'd gone light on her body, she'd gone super-heavy on her face, with makeup that completely changed what she actually looked like.

The teenager put her hand on her hip and struck a pose, catching her bottom lip with her top teeth, and exaggeratedly flicked back her super-straightened hair. 'Ag, Ma, don't be such an old bag,' she said. Terry could tell she was going for a buddy-buddy approach but because Rosanne's natural demeanour had become so persistently aggressive, it came out as both a criticism and a challenge – which, Terry thought to herself, it probably was.

'I'm not kidding. You're not leaving like that. Go and put on some proper clothes.'

'Seriously? Jesus, Ma, we're already late,' Rosanne snapped, all pretence at teasing friendliness gone. 'I am 17, you know.'

'Yup, but you're still my child,' Terry said, perfectly aware that was yet another 'mother phrase' that she'd sworn when she was her daughter's age (and similarly rebellious, although not as bad, surely?) never to use on her own children.

Rosanne narrowed her eyes and stared malevolently at her mother. It crossed Terry's mind that this kind of interaction sometimes ended up with the mother being stabbed to death in her sleep by the teenager, deranged by hatred and fury, and she had no doubt that was what her daughter wished for her just then. But whether or not either of them liked it, she was the mother, and her job was to make sure that her daughter didn't go out into the world half-naked, especially in the middle of winter.

As Rosanne turned and stalked off down the passage, Terry opened her mouth and then closed it again: she'd desperately wanted to add, 'And wipe off some of that eye makeup – you look like a circus act,' but decided to quietly accept having won one small battle and save her strength for fighting the war of raising a perpetually angry, recalcitrant teenager.

'As much as I don't believe that women who dress provocatively ask to be raped, that child is asking for trouble,' she said to her friend Nicky, who was sitting at the kitchen counter in the open-plan living area, nursing a glass of red wine.

'Young woman,' Nicky corrected her.

'Well, ja, but she's still a child to me,' Terry countered, and Nicky nodded and laughed. 'How come Jess never dresses like she wants the neighbourhood perv to lure her into his car in exchange for cigarettes?' she asked.

'Dunno. Some teenagers are rebels, some aren't. I got one that isn't.'

'You weren't one either, hey?' Terry said, and Nicky nodded confirmation. 'And I was, so this is my punishment,' Terry continued. 'If my mother was capable of understanding this, she'd have such a laugh.'

Both Terry's elderly parents were in a care home in the city, about a hundred kilometres to the south, and both were pretty far down the rocky road of dementia. Growing up, Terry had adored her father, an environmental scientist with a quick wit and a talent for storytelling; it was hard to believe the shrunken, confused, monosyllabic man she occasionally visited in the home was the same person. And, once her terrible teen years were behind her, Terry had come to admire her mother, who she'd finally recognised as a woman of unusual patience and compassion. Now, Terry's mom didn't know who she was, and the only emotion left in her arsenal seemed to be a kind of jagged-edged tetchiness. Perhaps she had a reservoir of it because she'd used so little of it during the lucid, productive years of her life.

Terry sighed and Nicky shot her a sympathetic look.

The slightly uncomfortable moment was broken as Jess, Nicky's daughter and her only child, came into the room.

'Talk of the devil,' Nicky said, beaming.

Terry looked at Jess with envy. Where Rosanne was loud and abrasive, Jess was quiet and kind; and where Rosanne was wild and difficult, Jess was calm and cooperative. And, tonight, where Rosanne wore a skirt so short you could see her panties, and a near-pornographic black lace bra under a sheer white vest – in the middle of one of the worst winters on record in this neck of the woods – Jess wore a hippie-style dress with a tight-fitting long-sleeved bodice and a brightly patterned ankle-length skirt with a lovely little flare.

'What're you two witches cooking up?' Jess said, grinning at them both. Without waiting for an answer, she added, 'Ah, can't we have a glass of wine?'

'No, you're driving,' Nicky said.

'Annie's driving, not me,' Jess said.

'Rosanne's not driving,' Terry said immediately. 'She's only got her learner's. You're the properly licensed one – you must drive.'

'Learners have to practise,' said Jess. From her, it sounded reasonable, Terry noted. From Rosanne, it would have sounded like whining.

Teaching Rosanne to drive had aged Terry about a thousand years. Her daughter's impetuous, impatient nature made her a challenging pupil, and the process had been hard on her precious Toyota Corolla, which already had several new scratches and dings to attest to Rosanne's erratic driving. The Corolla was the first brand-new car Terry had ever owned, bought just a few years before, with her own hard-earned money.

Rosanne enthusiastically brought her very big personality to bear behind the wheel, and always drove far too fast and with a belligerence that at times was really quite unnerving, with all the hallmarks of a young driver with absolutely no experience and zero grasp of her own mortality. Every practice drive ended up with one or the other of them in tears or screaming, or both.

'No offence, but I don't want Annie driving my car,' Nicky said.

'No, I get it,' said Terry. 'In a perfect world, she wouldn't be driving my car either.'

'Okay, so you're driving, so no wine,' Nicky said, gesturing at Jess with her glass. 'You're too young, anyway.'

'I'm 18, Ma,' Jess said. 'It's perfectly legal.'

'You may be an adult in the eyes of the law but in mine you're still my baby,' Nicky responded.

Jess made a joke sucking sound, as if she were mouthing a dummy, and she and her mother laughed. The atmosphere between the two was light and loving, and Terry found herself once again committing the deadly sin of envy. When exactly, she wondered, had that beautiful bond that had been so strong between her and her only daughter begun fraying, and how much more abuse could it take before it snapped?

Rosanne came back into the room, now wearing very tight jeans with tears at the bum and knees. She'd also replaced the Doc Marten-type lace-ups she'd been wearing with pointy-toed high-heeled black boots that would've made a dominatrix proud. And, for god's sake, had she actually added some more eye makeup?

Pick your battles, Terry reminded herself. Brightly, she asked her daughter, 'So, where are you off to tonight?'

'Farm party,' Rosanne said. She didn't make eye contact with her mother. Instead, she did a twirl in front of the reflective glass of the big wall unit on the far side of the room, and blew an exaggeratedly provocative kiss at herself.

'Whose farm party?' Terry asked, going for a light and breezy tone but hearing the poorly disguised interrogation in her voice. And here we go, she thought: squeezing blood from a stone.

'Someone from school.'

'Who from school?'

Rosanne made a grating noise in her throat and snapped, 'Ryan, okay?'

It definitely wasn't okay. Ryan was the latest in the string of eminently unsuitable boyfriends Rosanne had acquired and jettisoned over the last couple of years, and he was probably the least likable of the lot so far, which really was saying something. A hulking, brooding mass of a young man, he seemed incapable of normal human speech and limited himself to simian grunts in response to questions – if he even bothered to acknowledge being addressed. But if there was one hard lesson Terry had learnt, it was that the more she railed against the nasty boyfriends, the tighter Rosanne clung to them.

'Will his father be there?'

'Ma, we're not children, okay?' Rosanne said.

Ja, Terry thought, you're teenagers, and that's a lot worse than children when it comes to making decisions that will keep you alive and happy.

'Don't worry, Terry, I'll be with her,' Jess said, flashing a friendly grin. That was another thing about this enviably obedient young woman: she unashamedly took the adult role in her and Rosanne's relationship – and, even more remarkably, Rosanne seemed okay with it.

'Ja, Jess will look after me,' Rosanne said, slinging her left arm around the neck of the person who'd been her very best friend from practically the minute they had met when they were both 8 years old.

'When will you be home?' Terry asked, looking pointedly at Jess, instead of at her own daughter.

'When the party's over,' Rosanne said and gave her mom what almost passed for a cheeky smile. And just for an instant, Terry caught a glimpse of the loving little girl, her 'precious rosebud', who not so long ago had wanted nothing more than to please her mommy, and who was now locked somewhere behind the panda-like eye makeup and brittle façade.

'Mm-mm,' Nicky interjected, shaking her head. 'One o'clock. And we'll be waiting up for you.'

Terry shot Nicky a 'thank you' look. Rosanne would have kicked up a huge fuss if she'd been the one laying down the curfew, but she wouldn't challenge Nicky.

'God, you guys, weren't you ever young?' Rosanne moaned, but she didn't take it any further: a tacit acknowledgement of the girls' deadline.

'Okay, let's get going,' Jess said to Rosanne.

'You got extra warm stuff? It's going to be very wet out there again tonight,' Nicky said.

Jess nodded, slinging a duffel bag over her shoulder, and Rosanne followed suit, her old school satchel bulging with god knows what.

'Please take it easy on the road,' Nicky said to Jess, handing her the keys to her little red Ford Fiesta. 'I know you're a careful driver but it's raining and …'

'"… It's not you, it's the other nitwits on the road".' Jess repeated what her mother always said. 'Ja, I know, Ma. I promise to drive safely.'

The two hugged warmly.

Terry gave Rosanne a quick hug, feeling her daughter's body tense unwillingly in her arms and trying to quell the sharp little shot of pain this caused her. 'Have a good time,' she said. It took an almost superhuman effort not to add, 'And please be careful.'

Jess opened the front door and a squall of rain blew in. 'It's filthy out there,' she said, then she was swallowed by the darkness, Rosanne on her heels.

'You know Annie's got that tiny skirt in that tatty satchel of hers, hey?' Nicky said to her friend as the door closed behind the girls.

3

'Want another glass of wine?' Nicky asked Terry, waving the half-empty bottle of red. They had finished the dinner Terry had prepared some time before, and she was sitting at the kitchen counter, watching her friend tidy up.

'Ja, I do, but I don't think I should,' Terry said, glancing up at the kitchen clock. 'It's eleven o'clock. If the girls need a lift home or anything happens, I want to be sober.'

'You're such a worrier,' Nicky said. 'They'll be fine.'

'You can say that – you've got the perfect daughter,' Terry said. 'I'm the one with satan's spawn.'

'Ag, she's not so bad,' Nicky said, but not even trying to be convincing.

'*You* have her, then,' Terry responded, and when Nicky vehemently shook her head, they both laughed.

'I'm finding it all so exhausting,' Terry said. 'I wish she'd just get through her teenage rebellion already, and turn back into a normal human being.'

'They have to completely leave you first, apparently,' Nicky said. 'I read that somewhere. It's like having a crap boyfriend relationship. You can't go straight from boyfriend-girlfriend to being just friends. There has to be a long break with no contact.'

'Well, I suppose that could be next year, then,' Terry said, referring to Rosanne's recent acceptance at a good university across the country. This was somewhat surprising, considering how her schoolwork had deteriorated in the past year or so. It was the same varsity that Rosanne's elder brother Patrick was attending, but he would be graduating at the end of the year, so wouldn't be there to keep an eye on his tearaway sister.

'I don't know how to feel about it. I'm happy that she's going away to university, because it's what we *both* need. I'm starting to worry that if we stay together in this house for much longer, it's going to end in murder. But I'm also so damned worried about her. She's such a loose cannon, and who knows what might happen with nobody there who really cares for her?'

'Ja, it would've been better for you if Jess was going to the same varsity, hey?' Nicky said, taking a big glug of wine. 'She's a bloody good Annie-sitter.'

'That's not the only reason,' Terry said, aware of sounding defensive. 'They're also such good friends. Friendships like that are special.'

'Ja, like ours, hey?' Nicky said, and hiccupped, then giggled.

'Ja, like ours,' Terry agreed.

She supposed Nicky was her best friend right now. They had met when Terry's surprise divorce had forced her to downgrade her life and take her kids out of private school. Patrick, phlegmatic even as a child, had accepted this with barely a shrug of his shoulders, but Rosanne had never stopped complaining and blaming her. She'd had to put both kids into the local government school, which wasn't great but also wasn't terrible.

Her ex-husband had taken no time at all to abandon the country lifestyle they had once both so passionately professed to want. Leaving the kids with Terry, he'd moved back to the city. There, he'd married the bimbo he'd been having an affair with, and within a few months there was – surprise! – a baby. Jesus. It still gave her a headache to think about it.

That marriage hadn't lasted either – another surprise! – and he'd moved on to a similarly young but arguably better-looking model. He hadn't impregnated her but there was still time – he was only in his late 50s, after all, and Picasso had famously fathered children deep into his 60s.

Eugh. Terry shook her head as if to physically dislodge the icky thoughts from her mind.

Still, if her life had been suddenly and unexpectedly upended by the thoughtless behaviour of her former husband who couldn't keep it in his pants, Nicky had it worse, Terry reckoned. *Her* husband had inconsiderately died on her, leaving her with an 8-year-old and a pile of debt. Nicky, who had been a stay-at-home mom since Jess was born, was suddenly faced with a new reality, so diametrically opposite the one she'd expected to live that she'd never really come to terms with it. Being forced to find a job and pay her and her daughter's way in the world, with precious few qualifications and absolutely no experience, could not have been fun.

'Single moms, unite!' Nicky shouted suddenly, dramatically holding up her wine glass. 'You have nothing to lose but your panties!'

'As if,' Terry said, filling the kettle and turning it on. She scooped a teaspoon of instant coffee into a mug.

'You know, even if all the sex we had actually caused Phillip's aneurysm to burst, at least we did have all that sex,' Nicky slurred, referring to her late husband. 'Because, let's face it, I've had almost fuckall in the last ten fucking years.'

'You haven't done too badly,' Terry countered. 'What about that guy you met at The Black Cat?'

'Black Cat, Schmack Cat,' Nicky said dismissively, then looked puzzled. 'I haven't heard from him for a while. I wonder what happened to him.'

This happened to him, Terry thought, watching her friend begin her now-familiar process of unravelling. This is how it often went with Nicky. Occasionally she was the heart and soul of a party, who would dance on tables and then sleep with whomever was left in the bar at the end of the night. But usually a civilised glass or two of red wine turned into a bottle and sometimes two, and she went from being the most tightly wound good mommy on the block to a mess of tears and self-recriminations.

The Black Cat guy had actually begun as a sober connection, when a customer in the restaurant where Nicky sometimes worked invited her out for dinner. She'd been excited about it, and things had seemed to be going well, but Terry had known that Nicky's drinking would inevitably get in the way. It always did.

Right on cue, Nicky began crying. 'Fuck Phillip!' she sobbed. 'Why did he have to die?'

Oy, Terry thought. She took a second mug out of the cupboard, scooped a generous spoonful of instant coffee into it, then filled both mugs with boiling water. She added two teaspoons of sugar for Nicky, and plenty of milk. She put it in front of her friend and plopped a teaspoon into it. 'Here. Drink up.'

Nicky cheered up instantly. 'Ooh, coffee,' she said, delighted. 'You got any whisky we can chuck into it?'

Terry tried surreptitiously adding just a splash but Nicky saw what she was doing and exclaimed, 'Hey, Mrs Miser!' and jogged Terry's elbow so that at least a couple of tots made it into the mug and a couple more ended up on the kitchen counter.

After her whisky-laced coffee, Nicky had had another little weeping fit, and Terry had persuaded her to get into bed. She lived within walking distance of Terry's house but it was still raining outside, so Terry tucked her friend into her absent son's bed.

'Sleep tight,' she whispered, and kissed Nicky on the forehead.

''Night,' Nicky had muttered.

It was nearing 1 a.m. now. Terry was keen for the girls to get home. She wanted to go to bed too. She checked her cellphone a couple of times but there were no missed calls or messages about changing the arrangements, so she hoped she wouldn't have long to wait before they got back.

She also hoped Rosanne wouldn't call or text with new plans at the last minute. This had become a favourite trick of hers – she would go out, having agreed (however reluctantly) to be home at a certain time, then a few hours later she would send a text message to say that she would be back later. If Terry tried to call her, she wouldn't answer her phone, and no matter how many furious voicemails Terry left, Rosanne would stick to her new self-imposed curfew. It drove Terry up the wall, but Rosanne's defence was always that, just as Terry always insisted she do, she had *let her mother know*.

In the kitchen, Terry poured herself a glass of red wine. After three cups of coffee she felt a bit buzzy, and knew getting to sleep would be a struggle. This was another really crappy part of having teenagers, or at least a teenager like Rosanne – all the waiting up to make sure they got home safely. Terry had spent countless hours, some of them in a vortex of worry, waiting for Rosanne to come home. And, of course, her daughter just felt that she was being 'controlling'. She didn't understand how viscerally scary it was not to know with absolute certainty whether or not your child was safe and alive.

Terry knew she was a worrier, as Nicky had accused her of being. But with a daughter like Rosanne, worry seemed to be the default emotion. Another thing Terry envied Nicky a little for was how she could just get drunk and fall into bed, oblivious, not worrying about whether or not Jess would come home on time, if at all.

Still standing at the kitchen counter, Terry took a sip of wine and checked her cellphone. 1.05 a.m. She considered putting another log or two on the fire, but because she was expecting the girls back at any moment, she decided against it. A house in their street had burnt down last winter after the inhabitants had stoked up the fire to keep the house warm, then gone to bed. It was a miracle they'd survived. She didn't want to take the chance.

She gave the kitchen a last quick check – everything was tidied away – and took her cellphone to the lounge area of the open-plan room. Settling on the sofa and wrapping a blanket around herself, she switched on the TV and clicked through the channels to the news.

Rumours of corruption in government. The new president, who'd been in office for only a year, was proving to be the disaster many had thought he would be. Terry was a firm believer in understanding local and national politics, and participating as a citizen. She'd been appalled when he was elected. He had been formally accused of corruption and sexual assault before his appointment to the highest seat in the land. The corruption charges had been dropped (a political sleight of hand) and he had won the rape case. However, there seemed to be no doubt in many people's minds that he was guilty. Now he was running the country. 'Into the ground,' Terry muttered to herself angrily, and took a comforting sip of wine.

In the sprawling townships surrounding the city, shacks were being washed away in the torrential rain, or burnt down when those who lived in them left flames alight for warmth. Not for the first time, Terry thanked her lucky stars for her circumstances. She could afford not only the basics, but also many of life's little luxuries.

As if in response to her private thoughts, the rain began drumming on the roof again, and Terry looked at her cellphone. The girls were now twenty minutes late. She would give them until 1.30 a.m.

If only Rosanne wasn't so angry all the time, she mused. Some of her friends had either intimated or straight-out told her that Rosanne's rebellion was a reaction to the divorce, but she knew that Rosanne had been born with some kind of rage in her. It was like she hadn't wanted to come into the world. She'd emerged from her mother's body purple and screaming, and she hadn't stopped for the first nine months of her life.

When Rosanne was a baby, it had become so bad at one stage that Terry, exhausted and desperate, had phoned the paediatrician at 3 a.m., begging for help. She was genuinely afraid she was going to hurt this tiny scrap of furious humanity who just wouldn't shut up. The paediatrician had taken the unusual step of making a middle-of-the-night house call, and had put both Rosanne and Terry on medication – the baby for chronic colic and the mother for anxiety.

Well, thank goodness Patrick was such an easy little one, Terry thought now. She would have gone out of her mind if she'd had to deal with a ceaselessly crying infant and a difficult toddler at the same time.

Sadly, Rosanne's relationship with Patrick was also rocky now. She seemed to blame Patrick for anything that happened to her that she considered adverse in any way, from failed romantic entanglements to bad marks for school tests. It made Terry cringe when Patrick came home for a long weekend or varsity vac, and Rosanne got stuck into him. She could be such a bitch. And, of course, she, Terry, couldn't get involved. If she so much as opened her mouth, Rosanne angrily accused her of 'taking sides'.

She had to admit that Patrick dealt with it far better than she did. He appeared to be adapting to Rosanne's ongoing state of simmering rage, and sensibly didn't rise to the bait. He also seemed openly curious about Rosanne's apparent overnight transformation from a feisty little girl with a wicked sense of humour who worshipped her elder brother and loved nothing more than when he played with her, into this ticking time-bomb of discontent that went off periodically for apparently no reason at all. In characteristic fashion, though, he took it in stride. 'Hormones,' he would say, and shrug his shoulders. 'Just stay out of her way.'

Terry, as the mother of this walking, talking bundle of seething fury, couldn't 'just stay out of her way', as much as she really wanted to. She understood that simply because she *was* the mother, and the one person Rosanne trusted, she had to take all that abusive blustering, and still had to love her unconditionally.

'I do love her, I really do,' Terry said to herself, 'but christ on a crutch, she tests me.' Like now, she thought, looking at her cellphone again. The girls were officially half an hour late and she would have to decide what to do.

She dialled Rosanne's phone. It went straight to voicemail. Of course.

She dialled Jess's phone. Also straight to voicemail. That was less expected, and definitely more reason to be concerned. Jess was meticulous about keeping in touch with her mother – partly, Terry suspected, because she was quietly aware of her mother's drinking problem. It was completely unlike her to be out past curfew without having phoned home, as well as to have her cellphone switched off.

Maybe the battery ran flat, Terry thought. Jess may have been near-perfect in many ways but she was still a teenager, and teenagers' forward planning was notoriously poor. Maybe she'd just forgotten to charge her phone before they went out.

Feeling helpless, Terry opened the front door, stepped onto the verandah and looked up and down the road. The rain had eased off and there was a heavy mist. Terry could hear water still gushing down the street.

The night was very dark. The two streetlights, one on either end of the short block, weakly illuminated the road, enough to show only her car parked outside, snug against the pavement.

Terry stood in the cold for several minutes, hoping against hope that she would see the little red Ford Fiesta's headlights come around the corner, anticipating the mixed feeling of relief and irritation that so often accompanied Rosanne's homecomings.

Then she went inside.

4

'Nicky! Wake up!'

Terry turned her head away as her friend came to groggy consciousness, exhaling old-wine breath and coughing to clear phlegm from her throat.

'What? What's happening?' Nicky groaned. 'Oh my god, my head …'

'The girls haven't come home yet. Wake up. We've got to do something.'

Nicky sat up slowly, rubbing her forehead and eyes. 'What's happening?' she said again.

'It's Friday night … Saturday morning,' Terry said, talking loud and fast and as clearly as she could. 'You're in Patrick's room at my house. Rosanne and Jess went to that party last night and they haven't come home. It's …' she looked at her cellphone yet again '… just gone four o'clock.'

'Jesus. What?' Nicky said, sitting up and swinging her legs out of bed. 'Pass me my shoes.'

Terry quickly found her friend's takkies in a corner of the room and handed them over. 'What're we going to do?'

'Have you phoned them?'

'Ja. Both go straight to voicemail.'

'Jess's too?'

Terry nodded curtly and Nicky looked stricken. 'Well, we've got to go to the farm …'

'I went,' Terry said. 'Ryan's father – bloody horrible man – said the girls hadn't been there last night. Then he threatened to set his dogs on me.'

'What? Jesus.' Nicky rubbed her eyes. 'Okay. What if they had an accident?'

'I drove slowly both ways. I can't see that well but surely if there'd been an accident, there would've been some sign – debris or something?' Terry squeezed her eyes shut, momentarily overcome by the horrific thought of her child in a mangled pile of metal. Then she breathed out, opened her eyes and said, 'Anyway, somebody would've called us.'

'Ja, someone would definitely have phoned us if there'd been a crash,' Nicky agreed, tying the laces of her takkies. Straightening up, she said, 'Okay. The police, then.'

Terry took another deep breath and sat down on the bed next to her friend. 'Listen, what if they were just lying? What if they went somewhere else, not to the farm?'

'You're taking Ryan's dad's word for it they weren't there. Maybe he didn't see them. Maybe he's lying to you because … well, for reasons we don't know. And anyway, no matter where they were, we told them we'd wait up for them.' Nicky looked quickly down at her hands, with the grace to be slightly embarrassed – she sure hadn't waited up for her daughter. 'They'd know we'd be worried. They'd phone, surely?'

'Well, they haven't. Even if both their phones had died, if there was a real problem, Rosanne knows my number by heart – she would've borrowed someone else's phone to call me.'

'And if Annie hadn't, Jess would have,' Nicky added. 'She also knows my number.'

Terry knew the subtext was that Rosanne couldn't be trusted to do anything as considerate as letting her mother know she was safe, but Jess definitely would. But this wasn't the time to get into that, never mind how true it might be.

'Don't you have to wait twenty-four hours or something before the police will take a missing-person's report?' Nicky asked.

'In the movies, ja. I don't know about real life and I don't care.

35

We should go to the police now.'

'Okay,' Nicky said. 'Where's my jacket?'

There was only one vehicle in the police station parking lot, a cop van. But the blue light above the entrance was on, reassuringly.

Inside, a young man was slumped at a short bank of counters, his forehead resting on his folded arms.

'Excuse me,' Terry said.

The man jerked awake, sitting upright and blinking rapidly. 'Ma'am!' he exclaimed, clearly disoriented. 'Good evening!' He looked at his wristwatch and frowned.

'We're here to report some missing kids,' Terry said.

'Okay,' he said, making chewing sounds while swivelling on his chair. 'Let me just get the forms.' He leaned sideways, scooping a sheaf of paper off one of the desks behind him, and swivelled forward again. He was young – not much older than their daughters – and had an endearingly open face, with big brown eyes under a pair of dark, strong brows, and a wide mouth that looked as if it was used to smiling. He took a pen out of his breast pocket, and carefully wrote the date at the top: 'Saturday 24 July 2010'.

He looked up at the women. 'Name?'

'Mine or the girls'?' Terry asked.

'The missing children's,' he said.

'They're teenagers – they're both 17,' Terry said, as the man began writing.

'Jess is 18,' Nicky corrected her. 'Just.'

For the next forty minutes, the two women took turns giving all the information they could about their daughters and where they had been going the previous night. The young constable, Lionel Diez, wrote slowly, making many mistakes. His handwriting had started off almost illegible and, half an hour later, looked as if a beetle had fallen in ink then, half dead, had crawled painfully across the page.

Finally, Constable Diez wrote the last, tortured sentence of the report ('Mr Chapple said the girls wasn't at the party and said he would set the dogs on Mrs Branson'), put down his pen and flexed his fingers. Carefully lining up the four pages by tapping them gently on the counter, he stapled them together in the top left corner. Then he offered their statement back to the women to read. Since they had both followed his excruciating rendition of every word, they both declined.

'I need photos of the girls,' he said.

'I've got one from today on my phone,' said Nicky, quickly flipping through the pictures she'd taken recently and finding the one she was thinking of. It was perfect: it showed both girls, face on, in afternoon light, dulled by clouds but bright enough to show lots of detail. 'Can I bluetooth it to you?'

Constable Diez shook his head. 'My phone's old. It doesn't have bluetooth. I'll just take a picture of it.' Quickly and carefully he lined up the phone photo in his own phone's camera lens, and snapped it. He glanced at the result, then held it out for the women to see. It wasn't as clear as the original, obviously, but it was good enough for identification purposes.

'What now?' Terry asked.

'Sergeant Cupido is due in at eight o'clock,' Diez said, walking over to a roster taped to the wall. 'She's the detective. She'll call you.'

Terry looked at her cellphone. 'It's just gone six. Can't we wait for her?'

The constable looked pointedly at his wristwatch. It would be a two-hour wait, but he shrugged and nodded. 'She's often in early, anyway,' he said. 'You can wait there.' He pointed at a row of benches facing the counters.

As they sat down, Nicky said, 'But what if the girls come home while we're here?'

Terry nodded. 'Okay, one of us must go back and wait at the house. Do you want to or should I?'

'I've got a bloody awful hangover,' Nicky admitted. 'Let me go. I'm not coping here, and I'll be even less use in another hour.'

'Fine,' Terry agreed. 'Keep your phoned on and charged. And don't go to sleep.'

Ignoring the indignant look Nicky shot her, Terry fished her car keys out of her bag and handed them over. Then, feeling bad, she gave her friend a quick hug. 'It'll be okay,' she said. 'They'll turn up.'

She was saying it as much to reassure herself as Nicky.

Sergeant Tamara Cupido hadn't slept well, and it wasn't only because her 'bed' was actually the broken-backed and threadbare family sofa in the minuscule lounge of their tiny two-bedroomed house. It was just as well she was a fairly short person. Someone with longer legs would have had to fold themselves in half.

Her parents slept in one bedroom, which barely had space for the old double bed they shared, and her younger brothers shared the other room, with two rickety wooden single beds pushed together into a corner. One of the mismatched mattresses had been gleaned, in surprisingly good condition, from the town dump. The other had been donated by a neighbour.

The roof of the home she shared with her parents and two brothers was leaking like a sieve, and the whole family had been up all night, trying to cope with the rain coming in – in her brothers' room, there was a mini-waterfall directly above one of the beds, and the two boys had had to squeeze into one single bed together.

She felt scratchy-eyed and irritable, and she was also worried about how they were going to manage repairs. Hers was the only salary coming into the family coffers right now, and it barely covered expenses. There was nothing over for patches, never mind a whole new roof.

Outside the police station, she parked her old Mazda 323 next to the battered police van – the only one the station could use at the moment. The other one, which was in marginally better shape, was in the local garage. Blown head gasket, the mechanic had said. Apparently it was serious, which was a problem, because there wasn't anything in the budget for repairs, and there was absolutely no way their station was going to be issued with a new van any time soon.

She climbed out of her car, slamming the door and locking it. Walking towards the station house, she remembered that Constable Diez had been on night duty. He was a nice young guy, eager to please, but not the sharpest tool in the shed.

The tired-looking woman sitting upright on the public benches inside the station looked up and smiled faintly at Cupido as the sergeant came in, but Cupido avoided her eyes and walked quickly past. She unlocked the door that separated the back section of the police station from the public waiting area at the front. This door could also be operated remotely by the staff, by pressing a button under the row of counters.

In this back section, there was a toilet and a tiny kitchenette, a small stationery and supplies cupboard, a bigger cupboard for the station's filed paperwork, and the evidence lockup, which was actually a large metal two-door cupboard secured with a padlock. And all of this was separated, in turn, by a door from what they called the 'admin area', which was the space separated by the row of counters from the 'public area'.

Cupido switched on the kettle and scooped coffee/chicory and several teaspoons of sugar into a mug. She waited, rubbing her eyes with the thumb and middle finger of one hand, while the kettle boiled, then topped up the cup and added milk. Stirring it, she walked into the admin area and nodded at Diez, who smiled and nodded back.

Glancing across the counter, she greeted the waiting woman, who immediately jumped up, came over to the counter and began talking at the same time as Diez did.

Cupido held up her free hand, indicating 'stop', traffic-cop style. 'One at a time,' she said, then turned to the woman. 'If you don't mind, I just want a quick sit-rep from the constable here, then we can chat.'

The woman nodded but remained standing where she was.

'Um, it's actually about her case,' Diez said, uncertainly. 'Her daughter and her friend are missing.'

'Mm-hm,' Cupido held out her hand. 'Report?'

Diez turned and snatched the painstakingly written statement off the counter. He handed it to the detective, who put down her coffee to take it with both hands. She scanned it, turning the pages quickly and wincing inside at the myriad errors (maybe there was a course they could send Diez on), then turned to the woman, 'Are you Mrs Bronson or Mrs Hallett?'

'Bronson. Terry Bronson. My daughter is Rosanne ... Annie.'

Cupido could see she was holding back tears. 'Okay. Diez, get Mrs Bronson some coffee.' She turned back to the distraught woman. 'It's awful but it's better than nothing,' she said. 'How do you have it?'

'Black, no sugar,' Terry said.

'Ooh, ouch,' the detective said, and both women managed a smile. 'Come through the door there,' Cupido continued, pointing, and pressing the unlock button under the counter. She heard the click of the lock releasing, and waited for Terry to appear in the admin area behind the counters. Up close, Cupido noted that she was tall – at least a couple of heads taller than her, although that wasn't hard.

Sitting in Constable Diez's chair, Cupido gestured to the chair on the opposite side of the desk. 'Have a seat,' she said. Watching Terry with steady brown eyes, the detective took in her shiny brown hair cut in a neat shoulder-length bob, and her expensive-looking coat. She put Terry in her late 30s, maybe early 40s, and noted her smooth, clear complexion – something the police sergeant knew took care and money. She also noted the manicured fingernails painted a pale pinkish-orange colour – coral, she thought it was called.

The detective took a sip of her coffee before saying, 'Now. Your daughter. You get on with her?'

Thrown by the frankness of the question, Terry stared at Cupido for a moment before saying, 'Well, she's a teenager …'

Cupido allowed the silence to hang for a moment, then said, 'But you get teenagers and *teenagers* …?'

'Ja, okay, mine's a *teenager*,' Terry conceded. 'One of the difficult ones.'

Cupido nodded. 'So maybe she ran away.'

'Oh, no,' Terry said quickly. 'No, her friend is the other kind of teenager – the … the not-difficult kind.' She couldn't bring herself to say 'the *good* kind'. Rosanne may be wild, but she wasn't *not good*. 'Jess,' she clarified. 'They were together.'

'Couldn't your daughter have persuaded Jess to run away with her?'

'No, I don't think so,' said Terry. 'Jess is very close to her mom. Mrs Hallett. My friend Nicky.'

'You guys all known each other for a while?' Sergeant Cupido asked, taking another sip of her coffee but keeping her eyes on Terry.

'Ja, for about ten years,' she replied. 'The kids went to the same school, and I met Nicky at a parent thingie there.'

'And is there a Mr Bronson?'

Terry made an impatient noise. 'There may as well not be. He's more than useless.'

'Does he know your daughter is missing?' When Terry shook her head sharply, the sergeant continued, 'How does he get on with Rosanne? Wouldn't he be able to help?'

'He barely sees the kids,' Terry said. 'He's got another family.' Clamping her lips together in irritation she added, 'He's on his third wife.'

'But still, maybe he ...' the detective pushed.

Terry held up a hand. 'Sergeant Cupido, let me explain something. My son Patrick, who's in his 20s now, at varsity, had a much easier teenagehood but he was also, you know, a teenager. He got caught shoplifting once. He stole some biscuits at Sweet Surrender. Mrs Knotwood called the police and they picked him up. They brought him here, actually.' She paused, looking around the little police station. The memory of the phonecall from the policeman on duty, telling her that her then-16-year-old son had shoplifted from the local sweet shop, still filled Terry with dismay. So did the fact that Rhonda Knotwood, the shop owner, had called the cops rather than her, Patrick's mom, who she knew quite well. But Rhonda had had her own things to worry about at the time, Terry remembered.

Returning to the present, Terry said to Sergeant Cupido, 'When the police called me, I obviously called my ex, Jonno.' She spat out his name. When they first met, she'd found the name, with its noncomformist disregard of the letter 'h' and hip 'o' ending, so cool and groovy, but now she regarded it as simply silly for a man in his 50s. Why didn't he just call himself 'Jonathan', which was the name on his birth certificate? She continued her story. 'But he didn't pick up and I left an urgent message for him to get back to me, because our teenage son had been arrested for theft – a big deal, you know? That was on a Tuesday. You know when he called back?'

Cupido raised her eyebrows questioningly.

'Friday morning.' Terry considered expanding on this. It wasn't even he who'd called back, but his secretary, to explain that Jonno had been 'tied up' all week in 'important meetings'. When she thought about it now, she wanted to scream.

'Hm.' Cupido nodded her understanding, then said, 'Okay. And Mr Hallett?'

'He died. Aneurysm.'

'Tough,' she said, with sympathy in her voice. 'Is Mrs Hallett coping okay?'

Terry looked at the detective. What had she intuited? Or was it just an innocent question? 'Ja,' she said, shortly. 'It happened a while ago. The same year I got divorced. Like you say, it's tough, but she manages. We help each other.'

'Okay, so you say that Rosanne didn't run away because Jess wouldn't have run away with her. And this guy,' Cupido rifled through the few sheets of paper containing their statement, then put her finger on the name, 'Mr Chapel, the father of the boy who was holding the party, he says that she wasn't at their place.' The sergeant took a breath and looked up at Terry. 'So what do you think happened?'

Terry held her hands out, palms up. 'I don't know,' she said. 'Rosanne doesn't tell me half of what goes on in her life. They could've gone anywhere – they could've gone to a club in the city …'

This thought had been circling in Terry's mind but she hadn't wanted to give it any room. If Rosanne and Jess were in the city, then that made it so much more difficult to work out what might have happened to them and where they were now.

'They do that often?'

'No, never. They're not allowed to. They're only teenagers.'

Cupido made a noncommittal movement with her shoulders that indicated that age didn't come into it. And she was probably right. Rosanne had been smoking cigarettes since she was 14, and probably dagga too, and there was no doubt that she was having sex with Ryan. She'd probably been sleeping with some of the other, earlier deplorables. And she loved to drink. So it certainly wasn't a stretch to believe that she may have gone into the city to go clubbing or whatever it was called these days.

'Sheesh,' Terry said. 'This child. I never felt old and haggard until she turned 13 and suddenly changed into this sneering, disapproving, critical, furious monster. It's just bloody exhausting.'

Can't live with 'em, can't kill 'em, the detective thought to herself. She'd read that somewhere, in reference to men, but it applied just as much to difficult teenagers.

'You have any kids?' Terry said. 'You look too young.'

'I'm older than I look but no, I don't have any kids,' Cupido replied. 'But I was a very rebellious teenager. Very angry. Very unhappy.'

'You've turned out pretty well,' Terry said, with a small smile.

'Ja. Most of them do. It's just keeping them in one piece during those years while they do everything they can to end themselves.'

5

'Sure, I can get a warrant, but I don't want to officially search your premises. That'll mean lots more cops, dogs, the works. We don't want that, do we? It'd be so much easier to just have a quick chat, you, me and your son.'

Sergeant Cupido was standing outside in the muddy road, leaning on the farm gate, her muscular forearms taking the weight of her torso, her spatulate hands hanging.

Ryan's father, Charlie 'Vlieg' Chapel, stood inside the gate, fuming. He had refused to put the giant dogs in the back, so the noise of their barking and snarling dominated, filling the air with guttural wrath, making it almost impossible to be heard, which was clearly the point. The man was holding both by their collars, one in each hand, and the dogs were twisting and lunging.

'That girl wasn't here. I told the mother and I'm telling you!' he shouted.

'It's not that I don't believe you, Mr Chapel,' Cupido shouted back, seemingly unconcerned by having to compete with the boerboels in order to be heard. 'It's just that this is the last place she said she'd be, and she hasn't been seen since last night. Maybe Ryan knows something – maybe it's something he doesn't even know he knows.'

The two stared at each for a moment, the stoic woman with her steady brown-eyed gaze and the irate fat man with the cartoon moustache and the muscular dogs twisting at the ends of his ham hands. It was hard to believe that Vlieg had earned his nickname for being in the flyweight division of the amateur boxing league he'd belonged to when he was a teenager, thirty years and the same number of kilograms ago. And while life hadn't been exactly cruel to him, it also hadn't delivered the fame, glory and riches he'd expected back then, when he routinely won every fight he entered.

Sergeant Cupido shrugged her shoulders, apparently in defeat, and began turning away. 'I'll get a warrant and come back this afternoon.'

'No, just wait,' Vlieg shouted. 'Let me put the dogs away.' He didn't want the police poking around here. Not every single car on the property had been procured in a one-hundred-percent legal way, and if talking to this bloody woman meant getting the cops off his back, fine.

Sergeant Cupido nodded. She'd expected his capitulation, not least because the red Alfa Romeo Spider with the black soft-top that she'd spotted in the back corner of the yard, half-covered with a tatty tarpaulin, didn't look like the kind of car someone might bring to a backyard mechanic for attention. She also recalled that a 1980 model of this very car had been reported stolen from a nearby town a couple of months before. In an area where most crime was petty, nicked expensive classic cars tended to make an impression.

Chapel manhandled the dogs to the back of the property, shutting them behind a small gate. They continued to bark.

As he walked back towards the farm gate, Sergeant Cupido let herself in.

'Wait on the stoep,' Chapel said. 'I have to wake up the boy.'

Not ideal, thought Sergeant Cupido. She wanted to get inside the house. But, as is the case with so many things in life, it was better than nothing. She stood stamping the mud off her boots, looking out over the front portion of the property. It was a kind of junkyard of car bits and pieces, but she also saw household appliances: several fridges, some chest freezers, a stove, a pile of old airconditioners. She could now see the half-covered Alfa

Romeo more clearly. It was missing its rear number plate, but looked to be in perfect condition. She felt more certain than ever that it didn't legitimately belong here.

Chapel came out the front door, banging it open hard so that it slammed against the house wall. He was followed by a young man who had his father's facial features but was considerably taller, and who would, Sergeant Cupido could see, very soon beat his father in girth too.

'Ryan,' Chapel said, jerking a thumb over his shoulder at his son by way of introduction.

The young man, whose mouth, like his father's, was naturally downturned, was rubbing his heavy-lidded eyes and porcine nose, and pushing his hands through his thick black hair. Stick an over-large ungroomed moustache on him and he'd be a dead ringer for Chapel senior. The younger version was wearing pyjama bottoms and had on a thick winter coat, but was barefoot. It was clear he'd been dragged out of bed.

Sergeant Cupido looked up and down the stoep. There were four wire chairs and a folding table at the far end, but it seemed they weren't going to be sitting there. Chapel was going to keep them all standing. He wanted this interview to be as short as possible.

'Morning, Ryan,' the detective said. 'I'm Sergeant Cupido. Your friends Rosanne Bronson and Jess Hallett are missing, and I just want to have a quick chat to you.'

'That bitch Jess Hallett isn't my friend,' the big teenager said in a phlegmy voice. Already a heavy smoker, Cupido thought. 'She's just Annie's handbrake.'

Sergeant Cupido nodded mildly, then said, 'Okay, let's start there, then. What's your relationship to Annie?'

The teenager leered at her. 'We hooked up, you know?'

'I don't know,' Cupido said. 'Let's assume I'm the total idiot you guys know most adults to be. Explain it to me in words of one syllable.'

Ryan's expression took on a cocky look. It seemed as if he thought he'd scored one, forcing her to admit grownups were idiots. Sergeant Cupido resisted the temptation to roll her eyes.

'We had sex, okay?' Ryan said.

'Did you have sex last night?' Cupido asked.

'Ja, but not with Annie,' Ryan said, and laughed harshly before lapsing into a short coughing fit that ended charmingly when he hoiked something nasty up out of his throat and spat it into the yard.

Cupido cringed inwardly. It really was a challenge to love people in this particular stage of their life cycle, she thought. It was probably fortunate that they moved in packs, all of them as clueless as each other, because who else could stand being around them? She glanced at the father, who was smirking slightly and looking somewhat proud.

'Why not?'

'She wasn't here last night,' Ryan said, his tone losing its smug edge slightly. 'She said she was coming but then she never pitched.' Using one of his huge bare feet, he kicked a loose bit of concrete off the edge of the stoep and added angrily, 'Not that I was waiting around for her or anything.'

If the first part of this was true, it was helpful information on two levels. First, if Rosanne had told her her mom *and* her friends that she was coming to this farm party, then the chances were higher that was exactly what she'd intended doing. Second, the sulky quality of this hulking teenager's tone as he said that she hadn't arrived told the detective that he'd been disappointed or humiliated, or maybe both, by Rosanne's non-appearance.

'So who was the lucky girl?' Sergeant Cupido asked.

'Huh?' Ryan said, a blank expression on his face before

understanding slowly dawned. 'Oh. Rhonelle, Renee, Ren-something,' he said and shrugged. He was putting real energy into appearing uninterested but Cupido could see something else there, just beneath the surface: anger? embarrassment? guilt?

'You're going to have to do better than that, I'm afraid,' she said. 'We'll be speaking to everyone who was here, so I'll need names and phone numbers.'

'Ah, Pa,' Ryan whined, holding his hands out in appeal to Mr Chapel, who'd turned his back on them and was now smoking a cigarette, standing on the edge of the verandah and staring out over the scrap-filled yard to the river beyond.

Sergeant Cupido, surprised but relieved that he hadn't interfered so far, glanced his way, and caught him looking at the half-covered Alfa. The stocky man and the detective then exchanged a glance – they both knew exactly what was going on here.

'Give them to her,' he said to his son.

Sergeant Cupido pulled up behind Terry Bronson's Toyota Corolla outside the Bronson house and killed the engine of the police van. She sat there for a moment, using a finger to go down the list of nine names of people who'd been at the party. Ryan hadn't known all the surnames (and, in the case of the young woman he'd had sex with, he claimed he didn't even know her first name), and he had only two of the phone numbers in his cellphone, but it was a start.

'It was going to be more people but the rain,' the teenager had told her, defensively, as if she cared how many people had come to his braai, and how this reflected on his popularity. They had braaied in the back, in the boma, Ryan told her.

Sergeant Cupido wanted to go back to the farm later with a search warrant and some backup. She suspected there was more to be found on the Chapel farm than one stolen classic car.

The front door opened and Terry Bronson poked her head out. 'Hi, Sergeant,' she called. 'Come in for some proper coffee.'

Cupido climbed out the van and went inside.

She could see that since she'd dropped Terry off at the house this morning, en route to the Chapel farm, she'd showered and changed clothes. There was no sign of the other woman, Nicky Hallett.

There was a fire burning in the Jetmaster-style fireplace in the corner of the large open-plan room, for which Cupido was grateful. She stood with her back to it, lightly stamping her feet and rubbing her hands while looking around. Nice place. Cupido reckoned she could fit her family's entire two-bedroomed house into the living area of this one.

This is the kind of place you see in magazines, when someone buys an old house and does it up, the detective thought to herself: picture-perfect, down to the tabby cat curled up, asleep, on the vast, pillowy sofa.

In fact, all the furniture was big. It looked new, and there was lots of it. No hand-me-downs here. Nothing gleaned from kindly employers or junk shops. And Cupido knew the interior décor would be called 'tasteful' in whatever magazine this house might be featured: neutral colours, with some bright accents, like the big landscape painting on the wall, alive with pops of red and green and yellow, and the big yellow cushions on the two wingback chairs.

She accepted the steaming cup of coffee, and took a quick sip, letting the hot liquid slip down her throat and begin warming her from the inside. 'Where's Mrs Hallett?' she asked.

'She's gone home to shower,' Terry said. 'She lives down the road. She'll be back soon. So what did Ryan say?'

'You understand that you can't be a part of this investigation?'

Sergeant Cupido said, gently. 'I know it's hard, but you're going to have to step back a bit and let me do my job.'

Terry nodded. 'Ja, but was Rosanne there last night?' she asked.

The detective's heart went out to her. She could hear the strain in the woman's voice and see the tightness around her eyes. 'Ryan says not,' she replied, 'but he was expecting her.'

Terry closed her eyes and let out a sigh.

'It's good news from the point of view that if he was expecting her, it seems less likely that the girls went into the city,' Sergeant Cupido pointed out, and Terry nodded. The sergeant put down the list of names on the round dining table and said, 'I want you to have a look at this. Do you recognise any of these names?'

Terry looked down the list. 'Ja,' she said. 'Freddie Patrizio. He's in Ryan and Rosanne's class. He's another box of frogs.'

Cupido looked at Terry and cocked her head questioningly.

Terry explained, 'He's just full of shit, like Ryan. And these two – "Renee" is wrong; her name is Rhonelle, Rhonelle Caron; and Lindie-Marie du Preez. They're also in the same class. I don't really know anything about them, though.'

'None of the others?'

Terry shook her head. 'But the school is big – they could be in the same grade. I've just never heard their names come up.'

Sergeant Cupido nodded. Three out of nine – ten if you included Ryan. Not great. 'So Ryan is a box of frogs,' she said, and took another sip of coffee before adding, 'Tell me how.'

Terry shook her head impatiently. 'Ag, the usual. He's a know-it-all teenager. He spouts rubbish that he's got off the internet, or what some friend's conspiracy-theory father has told him, and insists it's true. He doesn't like reading, and he's proud of that. He thinks only nerds read. He's lazy, and he's proud of that too – he actually boasted to me once that he's never done any exercise. Not that it takes much to see that he's going to be a very fat person quite soon. So, you know, ignorant, lazy, entitled ...'

'What was his relationship with Rosanne like?'

Terry made a gagging sound and said, 'It was mainly a device for pissing me off, I think. They'd lie around here, groping each other, even if I was in full view, making food in the kitchen or something. I wasn't surprised that Rosanne did that. Her mission in life has become to embarrass and infuriate me. But Ryan just went along with it. It was so in-your-face, such a statement that he just didn't give a shit about what I thought. Since my up-close-and-personal encounter with his father last night, I understand more about that, though.'

'So you don't know the parents?'

'Not at all. Rosanne made it very clear that she didn't want me to meet the father. The mother left ages ago, apparently.'

Sergeant Cupido made a noncommittal 'mm' sound.

'Ryan was also such a bloody liar,' Terry added, channelling her anxiety and frustration into the memory of the rude, sulky young man who'd treated her, her daughter and their home with such disrespect. 'When he and Rosanne first got together, about six months ago, he gave me this whole chapter and verse about how he was a born-again Christian and wasn't going to have sex before marriage. It was completely unsolicited, and at the time I thought that maybe he was genuinely telling me something about his belief system, but I quickly realised that he was just creating a smokescreen.'

'For what?' asked Sergeant Cupido.

'I could hear them,' exclaimed Terry. 'I could hear the bloody headboard of Rosanne's bed knocking against the wall! Jesus, I mean, did he think I was born yesterday? I knew exactly what was going on!'

'Did you speak to them about it?'

'Not him. I spoke to Rosanne. She said it was none of my

business, which of course led to a huge fight. Of course it's my business!'

'Is she on birth control?'

'Mm-hm. Has been for about a year. The mini pill. For her skin. She had acne. Patrick had it too, worse than her, poor thing. He was on prescription meds.'

Sergeant Cupido nodded, then said, 'I don't want to worry you, but I do have to ask: do you think Ryan is capable of violence?'

The thought seemed to stop Terry in her tracks. She had genuinely not considered the possibility that Rosanne may have been injured by Ryan. That kind of thing happened in the movies and on TV, not in real life.

'I don't know,' she said, finally.

6

Down the road from Terry's house, Nicky Hallett was in the shower, crying and cursing her dead husband.

'You bastard!' she sobbed. 'How could you do this to us?'

Although ten years had passed since that terrible day when Phillip had woken up with what he'd described as the worst headache of his life, Nicky felt as if she'd never managed to move on. She was still stuck in that hospital corridor, listening to the doctor telling her the unbelievable news that her 29-year-old husband was dead.

'But there was nothing wrong with him,' Nicky had insisted. 'He was a health nut. He was ...'

'Unruptured brain aneurysms are typically completely asymptomatic,' the doctor had said. 'There wouldn't have been any signs that anything was wrong. It was only when it ruptured—'

'It was only a headache!' Nicky had shouted. 'A headache! How could a headache have killed him?'

Some admin person, a woman wearing a blue tunic, had taken over from the doctor then, and led Nicky to a room next to the busy reception, closing the door behind them. 'Mrs Hallett, is there someone we can call for you?' she asked.

Nicky's mother had come to fetch her, and taken her back to the house where her daughter was being watched by her father – 'being watched' in the sense that the old man had the rugby on on the TV in the same room where the little girl was playing; Nicky's mom and dad weren't exactly devoted grandparents.

'You're going to have to sell this big house,' her mother had said, pointedly glancing around at the fairly comfortable if shambolic home she and Phillip had overinvested in. Without looking, Nicky knew her mother would have that 'I told you so' expression on her face that she loathed so much.

'Christ, Mom.'

Her mother had thrown up her hands and snapped, 'I'm just saying—'

'No, Mom! Not now!' Nicky had said, loudly. She'd managed to pull herself together between the hospital and home because she wanted to be a sane and comforting presence for her daughter, but she was holding on to her composure by a thread. Just about anything her mother said would be almost certain to flip her over the edge.

In the end, her mom had come through for her for the following two weeks while Nicky organised the funeral and tried to sort out Phillip's completely chaotic affairs. She discovered to her horror that they still owed the bank a significant sum on the house – more than the house was worth. Her dad had also stepped up, helping her sell the house, and lending her the money to pay back the bank, and enough for a deposit on another much more modest (okay, tiny and tatty) house, in this small town. It was cheaper because it was in a rural area, rather than in the city, which she'd always considered to be her home.

Once all that was done, within about six months of Phillip's sudden death, it was up to Nicky to just get on with it. To get on with her life in a place she never thought she would be, and without the husband she'd sworn to remain faithful to until death parted them – obviously never for a second expecting that to happen so bloody soon. And, of course, she had to be both mother and father to her daughter, who was also traumatised by the loss of her father and her home, moving to a new town and being put in a new school.

She'd met Terry at a parent-teacher meeting, and they had

ended up sitting together on the row of chairs outside the classroom, waiting for their respective appointments. Rosanne and Jess were in the same class.

'Why is it always the moms who come to these things? What about the dads? Or are they all as deadbeat as my kids' father?' Terry had questioned.

'My kid's dad isn't deadbeat. He's just dead,' Nicky had blurted out.

Terry had looked at her in sympathetic dismay. 'Oh, my god, I'm so sorry,' she said. 'I didn't mean to—'

'No, I'm sorry,' Nicky had said quickly, aware that she was sounding unhinged. 'It was a few months ago. I'm still trying to get used to it.'

'That's awful! What happened?'

And weirdly, for the first time, with this total stranger, sitting uncomfortably on a hard chair outside a classroom in a draughty school corridor, Nicky was able to articulate, somewhat coherently, the bombshell that had dropped on her little family that morning. 'He woke up with a headache – a really bad headache, but he often got headaches. He went for a run, which usually helped, but he said it was worse when he got back. He also said his vision was fuzzy, so obviously I was worried. I wanted to call the doctor but it was a Saturday and we didn't have much money. We had no medical insurance, and he said he didn't want to pay weekend rates and it could wait until Monday. Then a few hours later it all just went to shit. He could hardly walk or talk, his vision got worse …'

She'd phoned her mom and asked her – ordered her – to come to their house to watch Jess. She'd cut her mom's endless questions short with a '*Just get here!*' The wait for her parents to arrive had seemed endless, although it was probably only about twenty minutes, but during that time Phillip had started drifting in and out of consciousness.

'It was like being in a nightmare,' she had told Terry. 'Everything was going in slow motion, and I was completely helpless. My dad helped me get Phillip into the car, and they did all sorts of emergency things at the hospital, but he'd actually already died by the time we got there.'

Terry, listening with her hand over her mouth, had asked, 'What caused it?'

'An aneurysm,' Nicky had said. 'Un-be-fucking-lievable. I didn't even know what an aneurysm was before one killed my husband.'

It was the offloading, there in the school corridor, that had somehow bonded the two women, as well as the fact that their daughters quickly became best friends. They were both single moms who happened to live close to each other, and Terry managed to pull some strings to get Nicky a job as the receptionist at the local vet. It didn't pay a fortune but covered most of her bills. Nicky picked up a couple of evening shifts a week as a waitress at a local pizza-and-pasta place called The Black Cat, which also helped.

Raising children single-handedly and working left both women very little time for dating, so they became near-constant companions, too. They spent most of their time at Terry's house, which had two TVs (so they didn't have to argue with the kids about what to watch) and a generous-sized verandah for the summer, as well as a fireplace, all of which were absent from Nicky's little place.

Nicky stepped out of the shower and towel-dried her hair, then blew her nose very hard on a big wad of toilet paper, having run out of tissues, as usual. She took two paracetamol with a glass of water. She wiped the condensation off the mirror with the side of her hand and stared at her reflection. She looked cleaner than before her shower, but it had done nothing for the red-rimmed eyes and blotchy skin caused by a combination of hysterical crying and crashing hangover.

Always petite and pretty, she seemed to be shrinking and fading with age. Her green eyes, not so long ago bright and beautiful, had waned to a curiously muddy eau-de-nil, while her blonde hair looked dank and ashy.

Squeezing her tired eyes shut to banish the unwelcome reflection, she turned away from mirror. 'I've got to stop drinking,' she said to herself, not for the first time.

In her cramped bedroom, while she pulled various bits and pieces of clothing out of the wardrobe, she thought about where Jess might be. Pressing her lips together, she fought a feeling of intense irritation. She knew that wherever it was and whatever the girls were doing, Annie was behind it. It was another of her bloody harebrained schemes, and in the next few hours the girls were going to turn up, and Terry was going to do her usual rant and rave, take Annie's phone away, dock her pocket money, ground her, and none of it was going to make the slightest difference.

She herself would have some words for Jess, too. No matter how devoted she was to her friend, how *dare* she put her mother through this kind of worry?

Nicky quickly pulled on underclothes and jeans and a long-sleeved T-shirt, then the woolly socks Terry had given her last Christmas, and a big comfy jersey of Phillip's that she'd clung to after all his other worldly possessions had been donated to the local charity shop.

At the front door, she pulled on her boots, scarf and coat, and reached for her umbrella. It wasn't raining at the moment but that didn't mean anything. It seemed to have done nothing but rain for the last few weeks, and the weather forecast said there didn't look like there would be much slackening off for the rest of winter.

Then she headed back to Terry's.

'The good news is that they probably didn't go to the city,' Terry said, as she opened the door to Nicky. 'The detective says that the girls were both expected at that farm party.'

'Woah, back up,' Nicky said, coming in and unwinding her scarf. 'Which detective?'

'Oh, Sergeant Cupido. She's the detective, the one who's in charge of the case. She's been to the farm already.'

'What did they say?'

'Well, Ryan said that both Rosanne and Jess were supposed to go to the party but never turned up. And she – the detective – brought me a list of names of the kids who did turn up, nine of them. I recognised only three but she said that was a good start. She wouldn't leave the list but I've written down the names I remembered. Look.'

Terry thrust a piece of paper at Nicky, who took it and scanned the list of names. Terry had jotted down seven of the nine she recalled. 'I think this Lindie-Marie is in the choir with Jess,' she said, 'but I don't recognise any of the others. You?'

'Ja, I also recognise her. And Rhonelle Caron and Freddie Patrizio.'

Nicky handed the paper back to Terry. 'So now what? What do we do?'

'Sergeant Cupido says we're not allowed to be involved in the police investigation but she did say that we could make flyers and posters.'

Nicky, looking uncertain, said, 'They're going to turn up, you know.'

Wow, Terry thought: she was also tempted to just hope for the best but her practical nature told her that preparing for the worst was the right thing to do. The girls had now been missing for about sixteen hours. Clearly, something was very wrong. But Nicky seemed not to want to think about this yet, and Terry had enough to worry about without having to try to convince her friend that something truly horrible may have happened to their missing daughters. 'Humour me,' she said to Nicky. 'I need to keep busy. The waiting is driving me crazy.'

Nicky seemed not to have heard. 'Jess is going to have to persuade Annie that the best thing to do would be to come home and face the music. And then that's what's going to happen. And Jess is in for it too, because, you know, bloody hell ...'

Terry stared hard at her friend, her eyes narrowed. Nicky may be feeling fragile, she thought, but she was going to have to draw a line in the sand. 'So you're saying this is all Rosanne's fault?' she said, in what Patrick would have called her 'dangerous' voice – the voice she usually used right before all hell broke loose.

'Huh? No,' Nicky said. 'But, you know, Annie's a bit ...' She shrugged.

'A bit what?' Terry wasn't letting it go.

Nicky realised that she'd wandered onto shaky ground – of course, it's fine for a mom to criticise her *own* kid; heaven help her if she criticised someone *else's* kid. 'Look, let's not fight. Sorry. No, I'm not saying it's Annie's fault, because whatever plan they came up with, and whoever came up with it, they're both in on it.'

'Okay,' Terry said, with a conscious effort to keep calm. She walked over to the dining table and pulled out two chairs. She sat and gestured for Nicky to join her. 'So, let's think about it a bit. What would the girls do instead of going to the farm party?'

'Look, Jess really didn't like Ryan,' Nicky replied. 'So maybe she persuaded Annie that they should go somewhere else.'

Terry looked up at her friend, noting her swimmy eyes and raw, red nose, and her flash of anger was suddenly replaced by genuine empathy. 'Okay, so – where?' she asked gently.

'Maybe somewhere here in town,' Nicky said, throwing herself heavily into the second chair. 'I mean, maybe they both got drunk and ended up crashing at someone's house. You know teenagers – they can sleep all day.'

Terry glanced at her cellphone, lying on the kitchen counter beside her. It was only 11 a.m. It felt as if days had gone by. 'Ja, I suppose,' she said. 'Rosanne could sleep for her country, hey.'

'Jess too,' Nicky said, willing to at least lightly spatter her daughter with the same 'problematic teenager' paintbrush as Annie, if it would help not to estrange her friend. She just couldn't cope with that right now.

'I know!' Terry exclaimed suddenly. 'Let's take a drive around and see if we can spot your car. If they hit one of the pubs in town, the Fiesta might be there.'

The town was growing rapidly. Lots of the big empty plots had been carved up into smaller ones, and new houses had been built on them. The settlement was beginning to look more like a city suburb than a charming little rural town. Not only that, but the old houses that had gone for a song sixteen or so years ago, when Terry and Jonno had moved here, following their dream to raise their children in the country, now sold for real money. Nothing was cheap any more.

Nicky had been lucky to get the house for the price she'd paid. Terry had, in fact, had her eye on it at the time. In her new professional incarnation as buyer-renovator-and-seller of houses, it was the ideal skeleton on which to build, with wonderful old bones. But the house Terry had been working on at the time – a newer one, with fewer of the appealing historic features of the one Nicky bought – hadn't yet sold, so there was no cash.

Now, driving up towards the town square with Nicky in the passenger seat, Terry thought, a little unkindly, that if Nicky's house had been cheap back then partly because it had been in a state of falling-down disrepair, ten years on it was worse. Her friend seemed incapable of applying the imagination and elbow grease it would need to patch up the old home's tattered exterior and reveal its modest but beautiful flourishes.

When it came to the quickening pace of development in the town, Terry was in two minds. Flipping houses was much easier, of course, when there was a ready market for the finished product. While city people continued to want to 'move to the country', she had a steady stream of takers. And more well-heeled people coming in certainly meant more employment in the boutiques, specialist shops, restaurants and cafes that were springing up like hothouse flowers around the village square and in some of the stylish side streets. This was definitely a good thing in a town where most of the poorer folk had previously worked only seasonally on the farms, as pickers, packers and pruners, and spent months of the year in a state of desperate poverty.

However, the national road was nothing more than a simple two-way thoroughfare for the entire hundred-kilometre stretch between the city and the town, and beyond, all the way north to the border. It was dotted with varying speed limits, ranging from a frustrating 60 kilometres per hour where it passed the turnoffs to a couple of small roadside settlements, to a slightly faster but still irksomely restrictive 100 kilometres per hour in other places. Also, because it served as a conduit between the city and the border much farther north, it carried plenty of heavy freight trucks and lorries. As a result, it was often a challenge to drive, and sometimes downright dangerous.

Another self-limiting factor was that the town was entirely ringed by farms, growing mainly grapes and various kinds of fruits. This meant that as the settlement grew, it could never sprawl outwards.

With Nicky in the passenger seat keeping a sharp eye out, Terry drove around the town square, where most of the pubs, cafes and restaurants were situated. The Ford Fiesta wasn't there.

'Okay, let's go street by street,' Terry suggested.

Terry drove to the southwest corner of the town, and turned into the road running parallel to the adjacent farmland. They drove slowly, looking for the Fiesta. Many people still parked their cars on the street, but the two of them also peered into driveways.

The town was laid out more or less on a grid centred on the town square, and it took the two women about an hour to do the west-to-east roads. Several times, Nicky got out and looked around doors and solid gates or over walls, but she never spotted the Fiesta.

They drove back to Terry's house three times in case the girls had returned, and Nicky kept trying both their phones, which repeatedly went to voicemail, until finally Terry said, 'Please stop it. It's making me crazy.'

'But what if they've charged their phones in the meantime?' Nicky asked.

'Okay,' Terry said, sighing, 'but can you maybe just call once every quarter of an hour rather than once every minute?'

Nicky noticed the expression on her friend's face and nodded.

'Let's do the other way, north to south, and if we don't find anything, we'll park and ask around the square,' Terry suggested when they reached the outer northeast corner of the town.

An hour later, the women were more or less convinced that

the Fiesta wasn't parked at any of the houses in the town. They had ended their road-by-road search in the poorer part of the town, on the south side, carefully scouring the much smaller and more modest properties there. Nicky had craned her neck over the dilapidated chainlink fences and peered into the tiny muddy back yards. Most of them had been made even smaller by the construction of additional makeshift structures which were either rented out to people even poorer than the property owners themselves, or had been knocked up to accommodate expanding families.

Nicky said suddenly, 'I'm starving. Let's go get something to eat, and we can ask around at the same time.'

Terry, who hadn't eaten since the previous night, also realised how hungry she was, although it felt obscene to want to eat while their daughters were missing … maybe hungry themselves, or cold, or injured, or scared … No, she thought, I'm not going there.

She drove to the town square and parked the car.

'Let's not go to The Black Cat,' Nicky said. 'I'm so sick of that place that even the smell of the food there makes me feel like puking.'

They went instead into Karoo Daisies, a little coffee shop that looked out onto the square, and ordered toasted sarmies and cups of coffee. Nicky ordered a large glass of water, which she drank down in one go. 'Still hungover,' she whispered to Terry.

While they waited for their food, Nicky, who'd become friends with most of the staff of the town's various pubs and eateries, asked about the girls. Everyone was concerned and appeared more than willing to help, but nobody they spoke to had seen them the previous night.

The two women took their food to go and ate it quickly, sitting in the car. Then they spent the next half hour going into the few drinking holes, restaurants (including the one in the local hotel) and other coffee-shop-type eateries dotted around and just off the square, asking about the girls. Nobody had seen them.

They even put their heads into Sweet Surrender, the little outlet owned by Allan Knotwood, a man widely believed, and with good reason, to have got away (so far, anyway) with multiple child rapes. To their relief, only his wife Rhonda was there, sitting glumly in the corner of the empty shop. When Terry asked her if she'd seen the girls, she said, wearily, 'Oh, fuck off,' and Terry realised she probably thought the implication was that her paedophile husband had had something to do with their disappearance.

Terry raised her eyebrows at Nicky and discreetly shook her head. She was pretty sure Allan hadn't taken the girls – 'Not young enough,' she mouthed and grimaced in disgust.

As they walked away from the sweet shop, Nicky said, 'You're probably right that the girls are too old for that ghastly pervert but let's not write him off completely.'

7

'I thought so,' Sergeant Cupido exclaimed triumphantly, smacking her hand down on the file open in front of her.

It contained the police report detailing the theft of a 1980 red Alfa Romeo Spider convertible with a black soft-top. It had been stolen three months earlier from a private residence in a much smaller town about twenty kilometres up the national road.

It had taken the police officer several hours to find the report. Despite its relatively large zone of responsibility, their little police station was very low down on the priority list of stations countrywide, and their office supplies didn't extend to computers. Everything was handwritten and then filed according to the date on which the report had been made. Cupido realised now that this was probably the least helpful way to file them. Granted, there wasn't a great deal of crime in their area – although as the town's population grew, so did the numbers of people committing illegal acts – but she'd still had to scan through a good sixty or so reports before she found this one.

With a few exceptions, the reports were of petty crimes: thefts of bicycles and cellphones, sunglasses pinched through open car windows, pilfering of petty cash from small businesses which usually turned out to have been done by disgruntled employees. In the 'more serious' category of reports Cupido had waded through were three domestic violence issues; an accidental shooting (a farmer's gun had gone off while he was cleaning it, and the bullet had entered a labourer's upper arm, fortunately causing only minor damage); an ongoing war between neighbours over barking dogs resulting in two attempts to poison them; eleven car accidents of varying severity but no fatalities (seven of which had occurred on the national road on either side of the town); seven house break-ins; and nine vehicle thefts.

Of the nine stolen vehicles, only two had been recovered. The classic Alfa Spider was still missing.

'So getting a warrant and doing a search is now not just a nice-to-have,' Cupido said to herself. Checking the calendar, she saw that the magistrate was due in town on Monday. She had no doubt that Charlie Chapel had clocked that she'd seen the Spider, and she was absolutely certain the car would be gone by then, if it hadn't already been spirited away.

'Diez, I need you to go to the city,' she said. 'You need to get a warrant for the Chapel farm.' She tossed the file containing the report of the theft of the car onto the constable's desk and said, 'This is our "reasonable suspicion" for searching the grounds but tell the magistrate we need to look inside the outbuildings and the house as well.'

Diez opened the file and glanced through the report. 'So you think they've got this car?' When Cupido nodded, Diez said, 'What's our reasonable suspicion for looking in the house?'

Cupido was impressed that Diez had picked up on this little inconsistency. She knew that citing the missing girls wasn't appropriate – the Chapels had told her that the girls hadn't been at the house, and she didn't have a shred of evidence that said otherwise. 'If they ask, tell the magistrate it's a big house,' she said. 'Big enough to hide a stolen car in.'

When Diez gave her a sceptical look, she said caustically, 'Don't worry, they won't ask. Those guys – they don't know anything about what goes on here, so very far from the city. They think we're all country bumpkins, raising chickens in our living rooms and marrying our cousins.'

She was fairly certain that whichever judge Diez asked to sign the warrant would do it without bothering to read it closely, if at all. Before she'd eventually been given Constable Diez to supplement the staff of three (herself, an inefficient admin clerk, and Constable Marcus Linney, currently on leave), she'd been the one appearing before the magistrate to present cases, give evidence, or get various legal documents approved and signed, and she'd been treated as a halfwit every time. Initially it had bothered her, but she'd quickly realised this attitude of the city magistrates – that her entire mission was apparently to intrude on their time with her silly, trivial rural complaints – gave her a fairly wide latitude in the way she ran things out here.

She thought about the only really serious crime she'd dealt with so far in her two years on the job here – and that was before she'd learnt how to swing the city magistrates' attitudes to her advantage. A local 'businessman' (which is how the newspapers had described him when they got wind of the story) had been accused of sexually assaulting underage girls. The man, Allan Knotwood, had arrived in the town from who-knew-where and opened a little sweet shop called Sweet Surrender. In retrospect, the irony was sickening.

His wife was the co-owner and manager. Leaving her in charge of the shop, Knotwood regularly went on lengthy trips to supply various outlets with their homemade produce – chocolates, biscuits, cookies, and a wide range of sweets. While away he'd been procuring young – very young, in many cases – girls for sex.

What had begun with a single 12-year-old telling her mother about the cadaverously thin red-headed man who'd made her 'suck his thing' grew very quickly into an assembly of thirteen girls, the youngest just 8 years old, all from the poorer communities on Knotwood's supply routes. Creepily, his method of 'payment' to – bribery of – all these children was sweets and biscuits from the stash in his pale-pink panel van.

Knotwood had, to the best of Cupido's knowledge, kept clear of the local kids when it came to his illicit sexual activities. The complaints and accusations against him had trickled into her office from the surrounding towns slowly at first, then in a rush as word got out that someone had broken the dam of silence that most paedophiles rely on in order continue with their abuse.

Cupido had put out word that a file had been opened on Allan Knotwood, and that anyone with something to report should come forward. When nothing emerged over the next couple of months from the town's communities, Cupido assumed that Knotwood had been careful not to crap on his own doorstep.

The first warrant she'd been able to obtain from the city magistrate, to search Knotwood's van, home and business, had turned out to be useless. Either Knotwood had been warned ahead of time that she was coming, or he'd been in a similar situation before, because before he let her into his house, he had carefully read the warrant, then pointed out that it didn't specify that she could execute it at night. The awful man had exaggeratedly tapped his wristwatch – it was about 8.30 p.m. and already dark – then slowly shaken his head, smiled mirthlessly, and slammed the front door in her face.

In the end, though, the sheer combined weight of more than two dozen witness statements, including details such as comprehensive descriptions of the rapist and his panel van, which was unmistakably branded 'Sweet Surrender' in large swirly dark-pink lettering on both sides, had prevailed, and she was granted an arrest warrant for the paedophile.

She'd taken an outraged and indignant Allan Knotwood into custody at his house late one afternoon, around the time most people were returning to their homes after work. And she had to admit, even if only to herself, that she'd taken some deep pleasure in cuffing him and leading him out to the police van in full view of his neighbours and various passers-by.

Initially she hadn't been surprised at the attitude of Knotwood's wife, Rhonda, who'd undertaken tearfully to stand by her man. Many wives of men who committed horrifying crimes simply didn't believe it, and truly thought that some mistake had been made. But as the court hearings mounted up and the stomach-curdling details began emerging, including irrefutable and heart-rending testimony from little girls who described what her husband had done to them, and how he'd bribed them – with the confectionery his wife had made – to perform various sex acts with and on him, and Rhonda's attitude didn't shift, Cupido was at first puzzled, then incredulous. Now, she felt deep derision for the woman.

But that was nothing compared to the utter contempt she felt for the travelling magistrates who'd handled the Knotwood case. First, despite the seriousness and frequency of the crimes of which he was accused, he'd been granted bail without hesitation. Rhonda had secured the services of a city lawyer, who'd driven out to the town that night and bustled importantly into the police station, waving around the necessary paperwork and loudly demanding the immediate release of his client.

And there'd been four hearings since, the first three postponed for different and equally bogus reasons: the lawyer had had car trouble on the journey north from the city and wouldn't be able to make it; Knotwood had claimed he was being framed – by thirteen little girls from five different towns – and that he could produce a witness who would confirm this but needed more time (the postponement had been granted but, needless to say, the witness had never materialised); and the third hearing had been put off because Knotwood's lawyer was, he said, waiting for an important document, its contents never explained or revealed, which similarly had never made an appearance.

The fourth hearing, just two months ago, had been postponed because Allan Knotwood had had a heart attack (and Cupido was sure she wasn't the only one who wished it had killed him) and was in such poor health that he couldn't possibly attend. That time, a new date hadn't even been set and now, two years after the first little girl had told her mother what Knotwood had made her do, it seemed that the case would never reach a conclusion.

Cupido didn't know the reason for this. Did Knotwood, whose background before he turned up in the town remained largely a mystery to even the most dogged gossipmongers and determined contributors to the town's grapevine, have some sort of history with the legal fraternity back in the city? Or was this just a case of a certain class of men sticking together, or of poor children having no real voice or power?

Whatever the reason, Knotwood had continued to walk around, a free man, and Rhonda had continued to play the dutiful wife. Interestingly, however, the townspeople had made their own assessments of the evidence, and reached their own conclusions, and Sergeant Cupido couldn't help but feel some satisfaction when passing Sweet Surrender and noting that, during the week at least, they never had any customers. The Knotwoods' business seemed to keep limping along thanks to weekend trade from the city – people who didn't know the inside story – but Cupido didn't think that it would be long before it collapsed completely.

Cupido wondered if, when she'd first heard of Knotwood's alleged crimes, she'd managed the entire thing a bit more artfully – perhaps got the search warrant she'd initially applied for from the city magistrate, or been more aware of just how dismissively the circuit-court judges dealt with cases out here in the country and so been more prepared to fight hard on behalf of the victims – the outcome would've been different. Perhaps. Perhaps not.

She shook her head, ridding herself of useless regret. 'Anyway, it's the weekend,' she said to Constable Diez. 'You're going to have to bother the magistrate at home, and all he's going to want to do is get you in and out of there as quickly as possible.'

While Constable Diez got the paperwork together for the warrant request, Cupido phoned the magistrate in the city. As she expected, he didn't remember her at all even though she'd appeared in his courts at least six times on various matters over the preceding three years, including twice in the Knotwood case. He was also irritated at being disturbed on the weekend and wanted reassurance that it wasn't going to be a complicated or long-drawn-out issue.

'It's a search warrant for a farm,' the detective said. 'I think there's a stolen car there, and I also want to have a bit of a poke about the outbuildings and the farmhouse.'

'Fine. Make sure all the paperwork is in order. I don't want any dilly-dallying,' he said.

Sergeant Cupido gave Constable Diez the thumbs-up. 'I assure you there'll be absolutely no dilly-dallying, Your Worship,' she said, stressing his title while carefully keeping all trace of sarcasm out of her voice.

Even though the traffic on the national road wasn't too bad on a Saturday afternoon, it was still going to take Constable Diez a few hours at least to get into the city, get the document signed, and get out again, and that was provided everything went smoothly.

The rain had eased off, and the detective hoped it would stay that way for the rest of the day, which would make Diez's trip both quicker and safer.

Sergeant Cupido was aware that with every passing hour, the chance that Charlie Chapel had got rid of the Alfa Spider – not to mention whatever else incriminating may have been on the property – was rising. She'd annotated the request for the search warrant to ensure that it could also be served at night, as there was no guarantee that Diez would get back in time for them to execute it in daylight.

Cupido glanced at her watch: it was 1 o'clock. With a bit of luck, Diez would be back with the warrant around 4.30 p.m. Even so, the timing was going to be tight, as the midwinter sun set about an hour later.

The sergeant pursed her lips and thought for a moment. The next problem was personnel. She'd exaggerated when she told Chapel that she could come back with 'cops, dogs, the works'. The truth was that the full complement of officers for this town and its outlying areas numbered precisely three, with two vehicles (one of which was held together with spit and string, and the other was out of action), and zero dogs.

She phoned Constable Marcus Linney's cellphone. He didn't pick up – probably avoiding her – and she left a message for him, explaining about the missing girls and the stolen Alfa, and asking if he would mind interrupting his leave to join them that evening to execute the search warrant. 'Every warm body will help,' she added, then slipped in the expression she'd heard Terry use, and which she thought summed it up nicely: 'This Chapel guy's a box of frogs.'

8

Terry and Nicky were in Terry's lounge. They had just had another vicious exchange of words, and the air was thick with tension.

Nicky's fear and anger, usually usefully channelled into her feelings of abandonment by her dead husband, were now fuelled by several glasses of wine, and her friend was the target. 'But seriously,' she'd suddenly said, out of the blue, 'what is Annie's problem?'

Terry, who'd been busy going around closing blinds, shutters and curtains against the gathering cold and darkness outside, had half-turned and said, 'What?'

Nicky, sitting on the sofa, had given a short, dry laugh and waved her half-full wine glass at Terry, creating a mini-tsunami in it. 'I mean, is it you? Is it Patrick? Is it Jonno?'

As always, the sound of her ex-husband's name made Terry cringe; it beggared belief that after all these years, the mere thought of him could still create waves of hurt and humiliation inside her.

'What are you talking about?' Terry had asked, turning to face Nicky; and even she could hear the 'dangerous' tone in her voice.

Nicky, her wits dulled by the wine, had missed it. 'Annie. Rosanne. Your daughter. Your precious little girl. Your teenage monster,' she'd replied, flicking the stem of the wine glass in Terry's direction with each phrase for emphasis. Wine had spilled out, splashing into her lap, but she hadn't noticed.

'*Jesus*, Nick,' Terry had exclaimed. She's drunk, she'd thought to herself, trying to control her irritation; now is not the time. Her words echoing her thoughts, but with a different focus, she'd said sharply to Nicky, 'Can we not do this now?'

'Well, then, when?' Nicky had slurred. 'I'm sick of it, I must tell you, Terry. I can't fucking wait until the end of the year, when Jess can get away from Rosanne's toxic influence.'

'Wow, Nick,' Terry had said, walking across the room to sit down on the sofa next to her friend. 'Okay, first, let's slow down on the wine. And then let's wait until the girls are home safe before we start with the character assassinations, okay?'

'Don't fucking tell me what to do,' Nicky had muttered, turning her head away, and Terry had been struck by how very much this exchange was like the ones she so often had with Rosanne: Terry being the grownup, absorbing insults, holding onto her temper and trying to keep things on a vaguely even keel; and Nicky being the wilful teenager, unwilling or unable to communicate rationally or negotiate with any civility.

'Nicky!' Terry had said, a bit louder than she'd intended. 'Stop it! We've got to keep it together until the girls come home.'

'Stop calling them "the girls", as if they're the same, because they're not!' Nicky had suddenly shrieked. 'Jess isn't a spoilt, inconsiderate little shit. She wouldn't be missing if it weren't for Rosanne! She'd be at home, where she said she'd be!'

All at once, Terry had felt overwhelmed by the totality of her life. By having to make all the big decisions about her kids by herself, and knowing that if things went wrong, it was only her to carry the can. By footing the lion's share of the bills for two entire human beings for all these years, because her ex-husband was using *his* cash to feather successive additional nests. By the countless hours she spent in the car as mom's taxi, and awake at night nursing sick kids or worrying about money, and at parent-teachers' meetings and prize-givings and school functions. By waking up every morning and plastering a smile on her face and carrying on, when often all she wanted to do was run away screaming. And most of all by being the sole punching-bag for her teenage daughter, who seemed to loathe her with every fibre of her being, without any rhyme or reason.

Breaking the momentary prickly silence, Terry had said, 'You know what, Nicky? *Fuck you.* I'm done with your wallowing. I'm sorry Phillip died but he didn't do it on purpose. I'm sorry you have to work so hard at crap jobs to make ends meet, but you're not the only one. I'm sorry you're climbing further and further into a wine bottle to try to find a solution. I'm sorry your life didn't turn out how you'd planned but for *christ's sake*, get over it and move on!'

Nicky's eyes had widened. She'd seen her friend give similarly toned lectures to her teenage daughter but she'd never had this cold, cogent anger directed at her.

'And most of all, I'm sorry you think Rosanne's such a fuckup. I don't know why she's going through what she's going through, but at least I'm not blaming everyone else. I'm coping the best I can. It's driving me absolutely bloody crazy but I'm trying to deal with it.'

The two women sat uncomfortably together for a few more moments. The air around them seemed to shimmer with ill will. A log in the fire popped in the quiet.

'I think I'd better go home,' Nicky said, standing up unsteadily.

'I think that's best,' Terry agreed.

The chilly early-evening air sobered Nicky up a bit but still the path she trod back to her house wasn't entirely straight. She unlocked her front door and let herself into her cold little dwelling. 'The hovel', she called it. It looked even worse now, in the thin darkness – all the curtains were open and no lights were on, giving the interior a slightly menacing, very unwelcoming air.

Nicky stumbled up against the tiny hall table, fumbling with the lamp until she found the switch. 'There,' she said in an overloud, falsely bright voice, as the light flooded the little hallway. 'That's better.'

She went into the miniature kitchen, switched on the overhead light, a buzzy neon job with only one working tube that cast a sharp, unflattering glare. She put the kettle on. She wasn't going to drink any more wine. Not because she was making a sensible decision, but because she didn't have any. But I do have whisky! she thought to herself.

While she waited for the kettle to boil, she stood in the middle of the linoleum-covered floor, arms crossed, and thought about perfect Terry and her unbearable daughter. A few times over the last year or so, she'd tried to draw Jess into a conversation about Annie and what was going on with her, but Jess was an unswervingly loyal friend (of course) and always politely (of course) told her mom that she didn't want to talk about it. 'She'll work it out, Mom,' was about as far as she would go. 'She just needs our support while she does.'

Just like her dad – Jess was fair and unflappable, and those were two of the qualities that had so endeared Phillip to her right from the start.

To her surprise, a loud, wet sob burst out of her, then another. She let herself cry, loud and ugly, for a few minutes – after all, there was nobody around to hear her, nobody to care – then she wiped her eyes, filled a mug with coffee and whisky, and went into the tiny lounge. No fancy open-plan arrangements in this little hovel, she thought bitterly.

There was also no fireplace. Nicky switched on two bars of the three-bar heater and turned it to face her, then sat on the little two-seater sofa and sipped the whisky-coffee. It burnt going down, but in a good way.

She didn't regret what she'd said to Terry. It had been a while coming, but someone had had to put it out there. Rosanne was a horror story – defiant, rude, disobedient, aggressive, selfish, slutty… All the things Jess isn't, Nicky thought to herself.

She could feel the sobs building up again in her chest. 'Where are you, Jess?' she said out loud, the sound of her voice in the silent house sinister and shocking. Hearing it seemed to finally bring home the awful reality of the situation: her precious, irreplaceable daughter had been missing now for twenty-four hours, and nobody had even the vaguest clue where she might be.

Nicky stood up. What she most wanted to do was to sit here on this sofa, drinking until she passed out. But her daughter was out there somewhere, maybe cold, maybe injured, frightened, hungry … She felt she had to do something.

She walked down the short hallway to Jess's bedroom, switching on the overhead light and looking in. It was neat and welcoming. Jess had loosely tied a pink scarf around the overhead shade, so it cast a soft rosy light. Nicky had to admit that Jess's room was the only one in the house that looked as if the person who lived in it gave a crap: her daughter had done all she could to make this small space pretty and comfortable.

The curtains were a bit long – they had come with them from the city house – but Jess had actually taken the trouble to hem them. Nicky had just left the ones in her tiny bedroom across the hall dragging on the ground, with the result that their bottoms were now dirty and fraying.

The pure-cotton duvet cover was plain white. It had been a special request, Jess's 14th-birthday present from her. Draped over it, down to the floor, was a big blanket that Jess had crocheted herself, in the shape of a mandala, in cool shades of blues, greens and purples.

There was a fairly big round purple rug on the floor, covering the ugly grey-flecked wall-to-wall carpeting that had come with the house. Jess had found the rug at a charity shop and proudly told her mom she'd paid next to nothing for it.

The low three-shelf standalone bookshelf next to the door was packed higgledy-piggledy with school books, novels, stationery, CDs, a little jewellery box, and other bits and pieces – but Jess had somehow managed to make it look busy and interesting, rather than just chaotic.

Nicky doubted very much that there might be a clue in this room as to where the girls had gone. She was almost one hundred percent certain that whatever had happened to them had been thought up and stage-managed by Rosanne – but in the absence of anything else to do …

She stepped into the room and knelt unsteadily next to the bed. Lifting the edge of the mandala blanket, she peered underneath: one pair of shoes, placed neatly together with their toes facing out, a tennis ball and a bunch of dust bunnies.

She straightened up and leant back on her heels, looking around, then slowly stood up, using the bed as a support, and went over to the built-in wardrobe. It was very simple, with a high shelf over a hanging space on the left, and six shelves going up to the ceiling on the right. Jess's shoes were neatly stacked in two layers in the bottom.

Nicky stood eyeing the top shelves, which were too high for her to reach. Jess could probably just get her fingertips up there – she'd been growing taller than her mother for some time, a genetic inheritance from her dad.

Coming to a decision, Nicky went quickly back down the hall to the kitchen, grabbed one of the straight-backed chairs and carried it back to her daughter's room. She positioned it in front of the cupboard, climbed up and reached into the back of the top shelf over the hanging space, where Jess kept her jerseys and scarves. Nicky pushed her hand in under them and felt around. Nothing.

On the top shelf on the right-hand side were T-shirts, and Nicky repeated the exercise there. Nothing …

Wait.

Her fingers had grazed something hard. She pushed herself up on her toes and reached in a little further with her right hand. Yes, there it was – some sort of metallic box. Carefully, she pulled it out. It was one of those hinged rectangular tins that contained geometry tools – compass, protractor, divider and so on.

Jess was a fairly good student but her weak point was maths, which she hated. For her matric year Nicky had finally agreed that she could drop to numeracy – the 'standard grade' of this schoolgoing generation – and even then she wasn't doing brilliantly. Geometry wasn't on the syllabus, so there was no reason for Jess to have this, never mind to have hidden it.

Nicky climbed off the chair. Standing in the middle of her daughter's neat, pretty bedroom, she opened the hinged box.

She stared uncomprehendingly at the contents.

In the box was a little paper packet of razor blades. Two were lying loose. They both had rusty stains that Nicky knew immediately was dried blood.

In the box were also several small wads of cotton wool, all of them similarly stained to varying degrees with dried blood.

'No,' Nicky whispered to herself, understanding coming to her in a grim, cold rush.

Last summer, how Jess had refused to wear the pretty sleeveless tops she'd previously so loved, even on the hottest days. And how she'd politely (of course) but very firmly silenced her mom when Nicky had tried to find out why: 'I'm not too hot, Mom, don't worry about it.'

And how she'd also stopped wearing shorts or little summer dresses or miniskirts – she'd seemed to go into some sort of neo-hippie phase where if she did wear dresses, they were long, flowing ones; and she'd bought a few pairs of loose-fitting long pants in light fabrics, which she'd worn rather than shorts.

'Jesus,' Nicky said to herself, carefully putting down the open box containing her daughter's cutting kit on the top shelf of the small bookshelf.

She stepped out of the room, switching off the light and closing the door behind her, as if this act would somehow negate what she'd just found.

Jess's cutting kit was almost exactly what parents had been told to look out for at a talk given at the school about a year before – that, and teenagers who wore clothing that covered their arms and legs even when it was very hot.

'Cutting is this generation's anorexia,' the guest speaker, a therapist specialising in teen problems, had said, referring to how, in the 1980s when many of the parents present had been at high school, anorexia had swept through schools like an infectious disease. 'Eating disorders like anorexia and bulimia, and self-injury like cutting serve the same purpose: they help stressed teens cope with built-up emotions,' the therapist had told the gathering of parents in the school hall. 'Teenagers who self-injure often have perfectionist personalities, but at the same time they may have intense feelings of low self-worth. Cutting is a way for these kids to cope with anger or shame or sadness or loneliness or guilt. And there could be an element of physical relief from emotional pain – for some teens, they can't put their finger on the emotional pain, but physical injuries are specific, and they feel it's something they can control.'

Ironically, Nicky had ended up at the talk by mistake. The one she'd wanted to attend was 'The Single Parent and Teenagers', and she only really wanted to go to that one because she'd hoped there may be some single fathers there too. She was sick and tired of dealing with life on her own, and equally fed up with the one-night stands with man-boys that she inevitably ended up attracting. But, in typically disorganised fashion, she'd got the date wrong – the single-parent talk had been the week before – so she'd sat through a lecture about a teenage problem that she would have sworn blind didn't apply in the very least to her daughter.

Nicky stood in the claustrophobic hallway, her hand clasped over her mouth. How many times last summer had she felt smugly superior as Terry had lambasted her daughter for dressing in 'next to nothing' – teeny-tiny skirts, short-shorts that showed the globes of her bottom, spaghetti-strap vests that barely covered her breasts – while Jess always looked cool and put-together in outfits that didn't make her look like 'a baby prostitute' (Terry's favourite description recently of Rosanne's appearance).

What kind of pain was Jess internalising in this horrifying private self-harming ritual? What onslaught of emotions was she relieving? Nicky groaned and sank to the hallway floor, leaning her head against the wall. This was at least partly her fault, she knew.

She had to face it: since Phillip's death, Jess had been increasingly filling the role of parent in their relationship. The more Nicky fell to pieces – drinking too much, crying herself to sleep, missing shifts at work, getting into arguments with people, having sordid one-night stands with creepy men – the more Jess seemed determined to keep it all together, projecting resolute cheer and optimism, telling her mom that everything was going to be okay.

Sitting in the half-lit, confining, chilly hallway of their neglected little house, Nicky sobbed. 'Come home, Jess,' she cried into her hands. 'Come home so I can be a proper mom to you.'

9

After Terry closed the door behind Nicky, she put her back against it and stood there for a while, looking up at the ceiling. Jesus, she thought; I just can't any more.

Maybe it had taken this crisis to show it, but Nicky was on a one-way mission to wholesale fall-apart. They had all ignored it for too long – her steadily worsening drinking, her progressively frequent outbursts, the sleazily inappropriate hookups that happened increasingly when Jess was at home.

Terry shook her head and pushed herself away from the door, sighing. She had Rosanne to worry about, and one troubled teen was enough. God knew this wasn't about Nicky.

She put another log on the fire and moved Jasper the cat to the other side of the sofa, giving herself more room near the warmth and earning a dirty feline stare.

Rosanne had chosen the moggie's name. 'Jesus, Ma, stop being so closed-minded!' she'd snapped when Terry had pointed out the cat was actually a female.

Terry sat down and stared into the flames.

Their girls had now been gone for about twenty-four hours – well past the time that it was reasonable to think it was just Rosanne acting out or their cellphones had gone flat or been stolen.

But it was that little word, 'reasonable', that kept tripping Terry up. If there was one thing Rosanne *wasn't*, it was reasonable. Maybe she was hiding somewhere, delighting in the anxiety she was causing her mother.

But then there was the Jess factor. One way or another, no matter what had happened, if Jess could have, she would have contacted Nicky by now. It seemed Jess knew exactly how brittle her mother was, and there was just no way she would have put her through this kind of worry.

In her gut, Terry believed that Ryan Chapel knew where Rosanne was. She couldn't imagine what had happened at the farm the previous night but she felt in her bones that her daughter had been there, and that Ryan – and maybe his hideous father – had had something to do with her disappearance. Or maybe the truth was more simple: maybe the two Chapel men were really awful enough that they were giving Rosanne a place to hide for a while.

But, again, there was the Jess factor.

One thing that Terry was sure of: wherever they were and whatever had happened to them, the girls were together. That narrowed the field of crazy possibilities: Rosanne may have had absolutely no concept of either normal social boundaries or her own mortality but Jess was firmly grounded in common sense. Given what the young woman had had to cope with, between her dad's unexpected early death and her mother never quite having been able to step up to the plate of reliable single parenthood, it was quite extraordinary how grounded Jess was. Terry wondered how she managed to do it.

This line of thought brought Terry to a realisation that they needed to start to look at circumstances that made it impossible for the two young women to be in touch with their moms.

Terry shook her head hard. It was far too early to go there. Sergeant Cupido said she'd be busy on the case the whole weekend and that in the meantime, Terry and Nicky could go ahead and make 'missing' flyers and posters. Terry had been sidetracked but that didn't matter. She could make the posters now.

Rosanne had a framed photograph on her bedside table of her

and Jess, taken at a school swimming gala the previous summer. They were both in school uniform, which was a good thing because it emphasised their youth; dressed up and with makeup on they looked like young adults but in the school photo, with the fresh clean faces and the peter-pan collars of their school tunics, it was clear they were just kids.

She walked down the hallway to Rosanne's room and was slightly surprised when the door opened. Contrary to her explicit instructions not to, Rosanne had begun locking the door when she went out. This irritated and affronted Terry on so many levels it was hard to name them all but perhaps what was most irksome was that Terry had always stressed to both her kids the sanctity of personal privacy, and she'd never once snooped in either of her teenage children's personal things. Rosanne didn't need a lock to keep her mother out.

The feeling of irritation passed very quickly, however. With Rosanne gone, the overriding emotions of fear and worry quickly eradicated all others, pushing them out of the way and expanding to take up all available cerebral space. Terry knew it was important not to give in to these giant feelings of terror and helplessness; she would be of absolutely no use to Rosanne if she went to pieces.

She saw the photo she was thinking of immediately. It was slightly smaller than she remembered but it was nice and clear, and it would do fine on a poster.

She picked her way across the bombsite that was Rosanne's bedroom floor, strewn with makeup, clothing, shoes, jewellery, books, papers and bags. There were also lots of soft toys, many of them dating back to her daughter's not-so-long-ago childhood. Terry quickly banished thoughts of a younger, happier Rosanne with a pang that was almost physically painful.

The bedside table, too, was a junkheap of stuff: earrings, nail varnish, makeup brushes and sponges, hair clips and elastics, various pots and bottles of creams and lotions …

Terry picked up the photo and looked closely at her daughter's face. Free of makeup, and with her beautiful brown hair tied back in a plain ponytail rather than straightened so rigidly that it looked like sheet metal, Rosanne appeared five years younger and a thousand times happier. Jess more closely resembled her day-to-day self, with her frank eyes and open-hearted smile.

Terry quickly put the picture to her lips and kissed the photo. 'Come home, Rosanne,' she whispered to it, and immediately began crying, the tears springing hotly from her eyes, and her mouth opening in a yowl that sounded like the summer-evening catfights Jasper got into with the tom next door. She tried to control the tears and the noise but she couldn't, so she sat down on Rosanne's bed and let herself go. For several minutes she scream-cried, not bothering to try to stem the tears and snot, letting it all run down her face and neck and into her clothes.

Finally, the crying drew to a slow, shuddering close, and Terry glanced at the bedside table, expecting to find a box of tissues there. She looked around the room – she'd put a box of tissues in here only last week, so it had to be here somewhere. Yes, there it was, on a lower shelf of Rosanne's shambolic vast double wardrobe, almost tucked out of sight behind some other boxes.

Rosanne's room was a movable feast of god-knows-what. She was forever 'losing' things in the depths of its mess; and other things that she hadn't seen for months continuously rose to the surface and were rediscovered, often to her daughter's genuine surprise and delight. A box of tissues randomly on a wardrobe shelf wasn't out of the ordinary in this chaotic environment.

Sniffing hard, Terry picked her way across the room and pulled the tissue box from the shelf. Its weight was unexpected and she almost dropped it; immediately, she realised that whatever was in it wasn't tissues.

She looked at the contents that were visible through the oval cut-out section of the box, recognising what she was seeing but refusing to believe it. There was a large resealable plastic bag of round pills in a variety of pastel colours, all with something stamped on them – she could see a butterfly, a question mark, a fish and the Chanel-style two interlinked Cs.

Terry took the bag out and stared at it for a moment. It looked exactly like the photograph on the little leaflet the school had sent out a few months ago, illustrating and describing the various drugs that teenagers could easily buy, and asking parents to keep their eyes open.

A shiver swept through her entire body, running over her skin from the top to the bottom of her spine and radiating outwards until it made her fingertips freeze. She felt lightheaded and sick, and wanted to wail, cry and vomit all at once.

She slid two fingers into the tissue box, scrabbling around on one side of it, and felt some small bottles; when she pulled them out, she saw that they were also brightly coloured, one with a label that read 'Buzz Aroma', another 'Pop'rs', the third 'Bolt' – she'd gone to gay clubs in the '80s and she knew nitrous oxide when she saw it.

Terry took the tissue box back across Rosanne's room, stepping over the debris, and cleared a space on the bed. Sitting down, she turned it upside down, putting her hand inside and swiping it around to make sure there was nothing left inside.

Tipped out on the bed, in addition to the ecstasy and poppers, there was another resealable plastic bag containing little neatly folded squares of paper. Terry carefully unwrapped one to reveal a small quantity of fine white powder which she assumed was cocaine or perhaps some sort of speed. A third resealable plastic bag contained dried organic material – magic mushrooms. And there were six small resealable plastic bags of dagga which had been tucked neatly into one far corner of the tissue box.

Perhaps most worrying of all was the plastic bag containing about ten small quantities, individually plastic-wrapped, of a crystalline substance that Terry thought must be tik – crystal meth. It was the red-flagged drug on the school leaflet – cheap as chips, it was often cut, badly and carelessly, with additives like talcum powder or baking powder, creating a perfect situation for an accidental overdose. Intensely addictive, it could cause frightening behaviour changes, including psychosis and violence.

Terry couldn't begin to imagine the ramifications of what Rosanne had managed to cram into this empty tissue box. Where had she got the money to buy all this, who had she bought it from, and what was she doing with it? Was she selling it? If so, to whom and where and when? And where was she keeping the money? And who else was involved …?

'Ryan,' Terry hissed to herself. It was that fucking boy, she knew it.

Her mind was freezing and racing, dipping and swirling; she felt as if she were in a tiny, out-of-control plane that was plummeting to earth. This, of course, was the reason Rosanne had been locking her bedroom door; and the only reason that it hadn't been locked last night was probably because her dear impatient daughter was in a rush to get out of the house and on the road to wherever she and Jess had gone.

Looking at the little treasure-trove of club drugs spread out on the bed, Terry realised Rosanne's disappearance could easily be linked to this. If she told Sergeant Cupido, then when Rosanne was found, she would almost certainly go to jail.

Terry swore under her breath. She longed to speak to someone about this but there was no-one. Jonno wasn't an option, obviously. Neither of her frail and elderly parents had much of a grip on reality. Nicky – well, given what had gone down tonight, she wasn't exactly going to call her up and say, 'Hi, Nick, guess what? My daughter's a drug dealer.' There was no way she could worry Patrick with this. Once again, she was on her own.

She spent some time repacking the drugs into the tissue box, trying to remember what she'd taken out first, and putting things back the same way as Rosanne had had them – this girl who couldn't keep a bloody row of books straight on a bookshelf had managed to shoehorn this stash tetris-like into the tissue box in a way that almost impressed Terry.

Then she sat on the bed, the heavy tissue box on her lap, and tried to think. What if this pile of party drugs was the one clue that would lead the police to her daughter? She couldn't keep it to herself. She had to tell Sergeant Cupido. The most important thing was finding Rosanne and Jess, and getting them back home. Everything else could be dealt with in time.

10

'Morning, Mrs Bronson,' the detective said, as Terry opened her front door. 'How are you feeling this morning?'

'Like a dog's bum,' Terry replied. 'I didn't sleep much. I've got something to show you.'

Cupido raised her eyebrows with interest, and said, 'I've got a report-back too. Do you want to go first?'

'Nope,' Terry said. She was in no hurry to tell the police that her missing daughter was probably peddling drugs. 'Come in. The kettle is on.'

The rain had started in earnest again, and the buildup of water in the little street was making it clear that the stormwater drains weren't coping with the deluge.

'Jissis, it feels like we're all going to wash away,' Sergeant Cupido said, stamping some of the wet off her standard-issue lace-up black police boots before she stepped inside.

She walked straight over to the fire and held out her hands to warm them. Glancing around, she couldn't help noticing that the magazine-stylish house looked significantly less picture-perfect today, with several dirty cups and used tissues on the coffee table, the bright-yellow cushions lying discarded on the floor, and the kitchen counter awash with dishes. There was no sign of the cat.

'We raided the Chapel farm last night,' she said over her shoulder to Terry, who was making coffee.

Terry immediately stopped what she was doing.

'We found a kind of chop-shop in one of the outbuildings, and two stolen cars in a shed.' The Alfa that had tipped her off had, of course, been removed by the time she, Constable

Diez and Constable Linney had arrived at the farm the previous evening at 7 p.m. Diez had been held up by an accident in the rain on the national road, but the warrant had allowed them to search everywhere on the property, and they had spent hours doing exactly that.

Chapel had been contemptuous and cocky when only the three of them had turned up in the buggered-up old police van. 'Where's the dogs?' he'd jeered, but Cupido had taken great pleasure in wiping the smirk off his face as she carefully explained what the search warrant covered.

'That's not fair,' he'd whined. 'You've got no reason to search the outbuildings. Those girls weren't here. We told you that.'

'Maybe not, but I can't help noticing that spot over there' – Cupido pointed to where the stolen classic car had been standing just hours before – 'has an Alfa Romeo Spider-shaped hole in it.'

Chapel had stared belligerently at her, but he'd realised that resisting was just going to get him into more trouble. Linney and Diez were both young and fit, and all three of them had guns on their hips.

She'd sent Constable Diez to search one quadrant of the back yard and Linney the other. Both had several outbuildings to poke through. She took the house.

Linney had poked around the boma with its messy spoor of the teen party – plenty of empty beer and cider bottles, a couple of empty brandy and vodka bottles, some empty and near-empty Coke and Sprite bottles, and about a dozen glasses, several of them broken; empty chip packets; cigarette butts in their hundreds; lots of roaches and two empty bank baggies with a couple of dagga pips left in each; a burnt-out fire. But there was nothing immediately obvious there that he could link to the missing girls, and no sign that anything violent may have happened. He'd moved on.

He'd found a few stolen cars shortly afterwards, parked together like sardines in a can, under a carport at the far back right of the property, covered with tarpaulins and what was clearly freshly cut and gathered brush – laughable evidence of Chapel's vain attempt at keeping them hidden. Although all the number plates had been removed, Linney had compared the VIN and engine numbers with the lists they'd brought with them and made several matches.

At the same time, Constable Diez had discovered another barn almost completely camouflaged behind a high wooden fence festooned with black-eyed-susans in bloom. At a glance it had looked like a boundary fence, and Diez was about to walk past it when he realised there was a large wooden building behind it. Inside was a disorganised but clearly fully operational stolen-cars and stolen-parts business – again, the list had proved useful, especially when it came to the pile of abandoned number plates in a corner of the barn, about half of which had been taken off stolen cars.

'But what I found in Ryan's room was probably of the most interest,' Cupido continued, and then quickly added as Terry's head shot up hopefully, 'although it didn't have anything to do with the girls.'

Terry walked around the kitchen counter carrying two cups of coffee, and handed the detective one.

'Ryan is a drug dealer on quite a big scale,' Cupido said, accepting the coffee and keeping her eyes on the brimming mug, thus missing the appalled expression that swept over Terry's face. By the time the detective had taken a sip and looked up, Terry had turned away. She wanted to tell Cupido about Rosanne's involvement in her own time and way.

'We've known for a while – six months or so – that drugs are being sold into the primary school and the high school here. Tik is a particular problem because it's easy to make and it's cheap and it's very addictive, and the effects are bloody awful.' Sergeant Cupido took another sip of coffee. 'The school is cooperating in all the ways they can, and they've been helpful in sending out info and giving talks to parents, but what we haven't yet been able to get is full buy-in from parents to search pupils' bags. Some of them say it's an invasion of privacy, yada-yada-yada, and we can't go ahead and do searches until we get one hundred percent of parents on board.'

Terry nodded. She was, in fact, one of the parents who'd protested when the school had sent home a note asking whether parents would agree to the police coming to the high school and doing random search-and-seizures. She wondered now if things would have turned out differently if she'd agreed.

'So we haven't been able to find out who the source is, although we thought for a while that it may be one small gang, or maybe even one person.' Cupido paused briefly and gave a grim smile. 'We found the motherlode tonight in that farmhouse. It's huge,' she said, spreading out an arm in illustration.

Terry shook her head. Her stomach churned, knowing that her daughter was somehow part of this 'motherlode' and she was going to have to tell the detective that.

'So, only Ryan and Charlie Chapel live in the house, each in one wing,' Sergeant Cupido continued. 'Ryan has been using one of the rooms down his side of the house as a kind of drugs storehouse-warehouse-clearing-house – he obviously thought there wasn't any chance that we'd ever search the place. There was a fortune's worth of all kinds of party drugs there, and all in various stages of being thinned down and broken up and repackaged for sale – tik, E, coke, shrooms, you name it. The father knew, of course, although he flatly denies it …'

Cupido tailed off and looked at Terry, who was now staring at her miserably. 'What?' she asked.

Terry sighed and put her coffee down on the round dining table. 'Come. I've got something to show you.'

11

'Mrs Bronson, I've got to ask you to please stop contacting those people and let us do our job.'

'But it's been a *week*, and *nothing*!' Terry cried into the phone. 'You can't expect me to just sit on my hands.'

'I understand your frustration but you can't go around accusing people …'

'*But someone knows something*!' Terry bawled, cutting Sergeant Cupido off.

As much as the police officer felt for the woman, the situation wasn't tenable. She'd received four irate phonecalls this week, and she suspected more were coming. Terry had memorised most if not all of the names on the list of kids who'd been at the Chapel farm the night Rosanne and Jess had disappeared, and apparently she'd been making it her business to track down and interrogate each one.

'There's no evidence that Rosanne and Jess were at the farm last weekend, and everyone who was there agreed that the girls never pitched,' the detective said. 'As things stand now, the farm is a dead end. We're looking at other possibilities.'

Much of this wasn't entirely true. With Ryan and Charlie Chapel arrested and taken into custody, Sergeant Cupido had requested a forensics team from the city to do a sweep of the property, especially the boma and Ryan's section of the house. If there was evidence of Rosanne or Jess there, it wasn't obvious to the naked eye and would need a much more careful examination to find. Predictably, the request had been treated with casual unconcern, and the team hadn't yet arrived. So, while the source of the emotion may have been different, Cupido's frustration levels around this case were also high.

The second untruth was that they were looking at other possibilities. The reality was that all their investigations so far had led to dead ends, and at this stage there was really nowhere else to look.

Cupido had had a very uncomfortable phone conversation with the absent father, Jonathan Bronson, who had in fact turned out to be as useless as his ex-wife had said he was. He had immediately and angrily blamed Terry for Rosanne's disappearance, on the grounds that if she'd been a better mother, everything would have been different and better; and he had referred to Nicky Hallett as 'that drunken slag'. But when Cupido had suggested he drive the hour north from the city to the town so that they could have a proper, face-to-face, sit-down conversation, he'd suddenly become far less opinionated and cocksure. 'I last saw Annie about six months ago, when I had to call Terry to come and fetch her because she was so rude to the wife.'

Cupido confirmed this with Terry. Mr Bronson had indeed cut the weekend visit short, after 'the wife' (the third in a series, apparently, and not very much older than Rosanne herself) had complained to him about Rosanne's attitude towards her. He had insisted that Terry drive into the city to fetch her. Since then, Rosanne had flatly refused to visit him.

'Look, he's a worm, but I know he doesn't have anything to do with this,' Terry had assured the sergeant. 'Rosanne doesn't trust him at all, and she hates his new wife, and, anyway, the truth is that he just doesn't care enough to harbour Rosanne, even if she'd asked him to.'

Jissis. People, thought Sergeant Cupido.

She had sent the girls' details and photos to the city, to be added to the missing-persons database there. The plain fact was, however, that no-one was going to be actively looking for them in the city, and unless they turned up, dead or alive, they would remain nothing but a bunch of personal info in a file.

A few days ago Cupido had dispatched Constable Diez to spend a day in the town, patrolling the streets, looking into properties, noting what cars were parked where, and also questioning the owners of the various hospitality businesses. He'd turned up nothing except that the two mothers had done exactly the same the previous Saturday, the day after the girls' disappearance, and had similarly drawn a blank.

Cupido herself had spent half a day at the school, questioning any pupil who voluntarily agreed to help – the law wasn't on their side there, either, as they weren't allowed to insist on interrogating any pupil without their parents' consent and presence. She'd been able to establish that both Ryan and Rosanne had been selling drugs at the school but they already knew Ryan was, and after Mrs Bronson had shown her Rosanne's neat little drug stash, they'd assumed Rosanne was too.

She had impounded Rosanne's stash, and it was in the evidence lockup along with Ryan's much larger inventory. It was clear that the two drug caches came from the same sources, and Cupido's theory was that Rosanne's little tissue box was her travelling stash, which she would take to school or parties to sell. The sergeant had been compelled by law to open a docket on Rosanne in her absence, and Mrs Bronson's concern that her daughter would be arrested and have to serve time if and when she ever did turn up was, unfortunately, pretty much on the money. Rosanne's age – 17 at the time the drugs had been discovered, making her still legally a minor – could be a mitigating factor but still things didn't look good for the missing teen.

Sergeant Cupido had also set aside three early evenings in the week to visit the homes of each of the nine kids on the party list, phoning ahead to explain to their parents that two girls were missing, and hoping for cooperation. She'd received a mixed reception, from the outright hostility of Mrs Patrizio (single mom of three boys, of whom the large and loutish Freddie was the last-born; worked as a manager in the local chain supermarket; probably fed up to the back teeth with having to deal with the apparently neverending fallout of her youngest son's beginner-criminal antics) to the warm and helpful concern of three of the families, who'd not only instructed their offspring to answer all questions honestly and to the best of their knowledge, but who had in two cases also invited her to stay for dinner.

Eight of the nine kids had confirmed what Ryan had said: that Annie had been invited to the party and was expected but had never turned up. Jess, who hadn't been personally invited, had also been expected – everyone knew that where Annie went, Jess went too. A few years of experience told the detective that the teens were probably telling the truth. Although their stories matched in essence, they told them in a wide variety of ways, with quirky personal differences, which seemed to point to the probability that they hadn't been previously agreed on or rehearsed.

Unfortunately, the one kid she hadn't been able to question was the one she most needed to, namely Freddie Patrizio, who resembled nothing so much as a flesh-coloured Incredible Hulk. If something untoward had gone down at the farmhouse last Friday night, Patrizio – brooding, malevolent, intimidatingly big for his age – was the most likely to know about it. Sergeant Cupido was still mulling over how she could legally pin down the boy and pick his brains, but Mrs Bronson was making such waves with the family that it looked less and less likely that she was going to be able to achieve this.

'Mrs Bronson,' she said, raising her voice to be heard over the sobs coming through the receiver. 'You have to leave the Patrizio family alone. What you're doing is illegal – it's harassment. It's also seriously getting in the way of the investigation.' Sergeant Cupido paused and listened to the sobs for a moment, then, feeling heartless but knowing it had to be done, she added, 'You're really not helping.'

'But what can I *do*?' the woman wailed. 'I have to do *something*!'

'I understand how upset and frustrated you must be,' Cupido repeated, 'but you have to back off.'

Terry listened tearfully while Sergeant Cupido told her that she was impeding their investigation. She was such a mess of emotions: distress and frustration, yes, but also mounting fear – fear that got bigger every day, and was beginning to completely engulf her.

She managed to hold it together for long enough to say goodbye relatively politely to Sergeant Cupido, then she disconnected the call and carefully laid the cellphone on the kitchen counter. She desperately wanted to hurl the bloody thing across the room but she kept it on and charged twenty-four hours a day in case Rosanne called. It remained the one and only possible contact between her and her missing daughter.

Then she screamed.

Patrick came running down the hallway. 'What's going on? Did they find her?' he shouted.

Terry, sobbing and shaking her head, fell into her son's arms. 'No,' she wailed, 'and they're not *doing* anything!'

Patrick lowered his mother to the kitchen floor and sat down with her, rocking her and stroking her head. He felt totally helpless. There was absolutely nothing he could do to ease this terrible pain.

Down the road, in the little house with the leaking roof, Nicky sat in the dark on the two-seater sofa in her tiny lounge. Although she had a blanket wrapped around her, it wasn't enough to keep out the cold dampness seeping through the panes of the small window that looked out onto the concrete back yard. The three-bar heater was next to her on the floor but it wasn't switched on.

In one hand she held a framed photograph of a pretty young woman with frank eyes and an open-hearted smile.

In the other was a large glass, filled almost to the brim with wine.

Now and again, like an automaton, Nicky sipped from the glass.

12

Terry woke up. She couldn't remember having fallen asleep.

It had been like this for three months now, and the net effect was an exhaustion that was difficult to understand, never mind describe: it seemed to permeate every physical fibre of her being, and it lay like a dense blanket over her mind.

Some mornings, she opened her eyes and for a second, a heavenly split-second, it was as if her life was still normal. She was going to get up, wake up Rosanne, put on the kettle and start the day. Rosanne was going to go to school, and she, Terry, was going to get to work. If she was out when Rosanne got back from school, she was going to phone home around mid-afternoon to check her daughter was home safely and nag her to do her homework and feed Jasper. She was going to pick up something for their dinner on her way home, and cook it while watching the news on TV. She and Rosanne were going to eat together. After dinner, she was going to phone Patrick for a quick catchup. And then she was going to go to bed and read a few pages of her novel before she fell into a well-earned sleep.

But the almost instantaneous realisation that none of this was true – that it was increasingly likely that none of this would ever be true again – turned that heavenly split-second into hell. The gaping sense of loss as the terrible reality swallowed her never grew smaller.

Most mornings now she woke up to this end-of-days, frozen-hearted, razor-throated feeling of emptiness and despair.

She didn't know what was worse: that sublime micro-moment of believing that her life was still intact, followed by the soul-searing realisation that, catastrophically, nothing would ever be the same; or simply waking up to the harsh reality that Rosanne was still missing, and that with each passing day the likelihood that she would return diminished.

Terry checked her phone – no calls or messages – and noted the time, then looked at the light filtering in through her bedroom curtains. Summer was well on its way. It was getting light much earlier, and the rainy season was finally drawing to an end.

She looked with a dull lack of concern at the growing patch of rising damp in the corner of her bedroom. In her previous life, the one that had had Rosanne in it, she would already have done something to address this. Now, she didn't care.

There were other rain-induced problems in the house. The roof had sprung some impressive leaks, and in one of the bathrooms water ran down the interior wall whenever it rained. But she didn't care about them either. She didn't care if this bloody house fell down around her ears.

A few weeks earlier Jasper had absconded. The cat and Terry had never got on – even in a species known for snootiness, Jasper's superciliousness was as unremitting as it was unmerited, in Terry's opinion. That said, the cat's blanket disdain for the human race had, curiously, never extended to Rosanne, who was the only person ever permitted to pick her up. In fact, Jasper's favourite place had been slung around Rosanne's shoulders like some sort of living scarf. So, because Rosanne had adored the bad-tempered little tabby, Terry had found a tiny degree of comfort in the cat's regular morning and evening appearances, even if she knew perfectly well that the moggie was only pitching up to eat.

And now she too was gone. No doubt she'd also grown weary of living in a place with a Rosanne-shaped void where its heart used to be.

Terry lay in bed, consciously not thinking. She'd perfected

this art in the last couple of months – emptying her mind and staring fixedly at one spot for long periods of time. Thinking was painful. And it was dangerous – it tricked her mind into allowing her to think there was hope when there was none.

She was going to phone Sergeant Cupido today, as she did most Fridays. She didn't expect to learn anything new – the detective would have contacted her if she'd heard anything – but she wanted to make sure that Rosanne's case didn't go cold.

There had been dishearteningly little new information over the last few months. About two months before, a forensics team had done a close examination of the Chapel premises and had found Rosanne's fingerprints in Ryan's bedroom, in the bathroom and in the room in which all the drugs had been found. Some of her hair had been found in the house too. Terry had given the team full access to Rosanne's room at home, and they had taken prints, and DNA from her hairbrush and toothbrush to do a comparison.

But none of the discarded bottles and glasses and cigarette stubs at the boma had borne any trace of either of the girls. Sergeant Cupido had tried to convince her that this seemed to confirm the narrative that the girls had not arrived at the party, but Terry still had her doubts. Freddie Patrizio had never been questioned and she wondered what he knew and what he was keeping to himself.

Patrick had gone back to varsity now. Shortly after Rosanne's disappearance, he'd got permission from his lecturers to return home to support his mother. He'd helped her print up and disseminate the hundreds of posters and flyers bearing Rosanne and Jess's likeness and their personal details, walking around the town and stapling them to trees and putting them under windscreen wipers and dropping them through mailboxes.

He had also dropped a bunch off at the police station, asking

Sergeant Cupido to arrange for them to be sent through to the city. She'd said she would but there was no way for Terry to confirm this had been done.

Terry had felt panicky about Patrick going back to varsity. Although nothing concrete had been achieved in the fortnight he'd been home, he was another presence in the house, where Rosanne's ongoing non-presence was not just a passive absence but an active loss. The unusual neatness of all the rooms, bereft of the shrapnel of Rosanne's chaotic presence, and the dense quietness that saturated every space, seemed to Terry to be reproachful reminders of her daughter's disappearance.

In the end, though, Terry had managed to amass the self-control to put on a good enough front to persuade herself more than Patrick that it was fine for him to go back to finish the academic year. 'It's only until October,' he had reminded her at the airport as she kissed him goodbye. She'd smiled and nodded, but the looming weeks ahead without his unruffled and reassuring presence made 'until October' feel like 'until the rivers run dry'.

On the night before he left, Patrick had begged his mother to reconcile with Nicky. 'She's in a terrible state,' he told her. 'She really needs you.'

Patrick – calm, kind Patrick – had, of course, been up to Nicky's place every day, and come back with tales of how she was drunk and unwashed, losing weight, not speaking coherently, crying all the time …

'It's barely different from what she's like normally,' Terry had said. The tiny pang of guilt she'd felt at this grossly unfair and inaccurate assessment passed almost immediately: Nicky had made it clear that she thought Rosanne was responsible for what had happened, and until she apologised for the horrible things she'd said about her daughter, she was dead to Terry.

'Mom, seriously, I think you need to just go and have a look,' Patrick had said at the end of the first week of his stay. He had been taking food – food cooked by her – up to Nicky's every day but bringing the dishes back untouched. 'I think she's in genuine trouble.'

'She's been in genuine trouble for years,' Terry had said. 'Nothing I do makes any difference.'

There was truth in this – Terry had talked to Nicky a few times about her drinking, and had repeatedly tried to encourage her to fix up her house, with plenty of ideas for cheap-and-cheerful improvements as well as offers of her very willing hands. She'd got her the job at the vet (which, according to Patrick, she hadn't been to in weeks), but nothing about Nicky's situation ever really seemed to change. In the almost ten years the two women had known each other, Nicky's drinking had slowly but steadily worsened, and her house had as steadily fallen into increasing disrepair. The unsuitable hookups had also slowly become, if not more unsuitable, certainly more unattractive, as Nicky grew older and both her appearance and her standards eroded.

And then, two days before Patrick was due to leave, he'd come rushing back from a visit to Nicky's and told Terry that he'd found her unconscious, lying on the floor in the little kitchen. 'I called the doctor. He came with an ambulance and they've taken her to hospital.'

Still she couldn't bring herself to forgive her friend for the things she'd said about her daughter. Terry felt that if she did, she would somehow be betraying Rosanne. At least she'd had the sense to acknowledge to herself the incredible pettiness of this notion, but she didn't admit it to Patrick. Instead, she'd just stalled. 'I'll go, I'll go,' she'd promised.

But she hadn't, and now months had passed. It felt like too much water had gone under the bridge for her to try to make contact. Anyway, she told herself, she hadn't heard anything drastic about Nicky via the usually very active town grapevine – one that was in the process of being both bolstered, in terms of numbers and access, by the establishment of a Facebook page devoted to the town's various doings, and destroyed by it, in terms of the astonishing lack of manners or tolerance of most of the contributors.

'No news is good news,' she said to herself, thinking about Nicky – and then barked a cold laugh at the utter nonsense of that idiom when it came to the total lack of news about her missing daughter.

13

It was the second anniversary of the night Rosanne had disappeared. Terry stood next to her car parked in the Chapel front yard, watching the river flow by across the dirt road. She couldn't see the bridge, which was about a kilometre upriver, and around a bend.

Behind her was what remained of the Chapel farmstead: with the son and father both in prison, the house seemed to have been left to fall into disrepair. Terry didn't know the technicalities of what happened to a property when its owners were incarcerated, but in this case it seemed that it had simply been abandoned.

This was the first time she'd been here in the last year, but it wasn't the first time she'd been here since her daughter disappeared – not by a long shot. In the first year after Rosanne had vanished, she'd made regular pilgrimages to this damned place, looking fruitlessly for clues that might have miraculously led her to her daughter.

Last year, on the first anniversary of Rosanne's vanishing, it had been raining – just as it had been the night she'd gone missing. Terry had driven into the yard through the wide gap where the farm gate had been just weeks before – it was no longer there, and Terry supposed it had been scavenged for some other use. She'd allowed herself a tiny, bitter grin about the simultaneous disappearance of that stupid, ill-spelled sign ('Trespasers will be shot. Survivors will be persecuted') that had been wired to the gate.

She'd stopped her car in the yard, then got out and run through the rain and up the stairs. She'd stood under the shelter of the verandah, watching for several moments as the downpour began slowly transforming the yard into a wide, shallow, scummy pond.

It had been early afternoon, overcast and gloomy. Terry had learnt to bring a torch when she poked around in the ruins of the farmhouse. She'd also learnt to watch her step. A fire had been lit directly on the floor of one wing of the house in the months following its desertion, and it had done some pretty serious damage, burning through the ceiling and most of the roof above. On one of the first occasions she'd come here, she'd put a foot wrong in this part of the house and somehow dislodged a pile of debris, which had crashed down around her, thankfully not pinning her under anything.

She'd walked slowly and carefully through the house, using her torch to light the way, and exited through the back door into the big back yard. The boma in which the teens had partied a year before was to her left. She'd jog-trotted quickly through the rain and into the boma, where she'd discovered its roof, too, damaged by fire. She'd quickly pulled her foldup umbrella from her shoulder bag and opened it above her.

She'd shone the torch around. No sign remained of the party – all the bottles and glasses and other debris had long since been removed by the police or scavenged by other 'trespasers'.

Nonetheless, here – or somewhere very near here – is where Terry believed that her daughter had disappeared. She didn't care how many times Sergeant Cupido told her that there was no evidence of it, or how unsuspiciously unanimous all the other teens' narratives were that Rosanne and Jess hadn't been here that night. In her gut, with her mother's instinct, she just knew that the girls had got into some kind of trouble somewhere here.

Terry had taken a stout red candle and a box of matches from her bag. Balancing the candle on what remained of the cement structure of what had once been a braai, she'd lit it. Staring at the flame as it flickered then took hold, burning steadily, she'd whispered, 'Rosanne, please come home.'

She'd left the candle burning, and had not gone back to the Chapel farm for a year.

Now, today, on the second anniversary of Rosanne's disappearance, it was overcast and gloomy but it wasn't raining.

All indications were that this year's rainfall was going to be far less heavy than the previous two years', approaching what was more normal for winter in this part of the country. In fact, meteorologists warned that the region could be heading into a dry spell – which in the current soaking circumstances seemed to Terry highly unlikely.

A few other things were different this year. For one, Terry now believed that Rosanne was dead.

She'd reached this conclusion as a result of Patrick's ongoing contact with Nicky, who'd been in and out of various drying-out programmes, rehab facilities and psychiatric hospitals for the past eighteen months, before finally moving in with her parents.

Patrick had got a good job in the city, coincidentally close to where Nicky's parents lived, and he'd been popping in and seeing her occasionally, and reporting back to his mother on these visits, whether she liked it or not. (She didn't.) The reports were consistent in one respect: Jess, too, had not turned up.

Terry had to admit it: while the chance existed that Rosanne had run away, and remained a 'missing person' out of choice, there was no possibility that the same applied to Jess. There was simply no way that Jess would've put her mother through the torture of not knowing where her only child was for all this time. And the natural corollary – or at least one of them – was that Jess was no longer alive.

And if Jess was no longer alive, neither was Rosanne.

In her darkest hours, Terry knew there were things that could happen to young women that were arguably worse than death. But with no evidence of, for example, kidnapping or trafficking of any other young women in or around the area, before the disappearance of the girls, or since, Terry had slowly come to believe that Rosanne was dead.

How she'd died: well, that was a whole other issue, Terry had thought, as she'd parked her car in the now-familiar although even more decrepit front yard. She had got out, standing for a few moments and staring across the dirt road at the river. Then she turned and looked up at what remained of the farmhouse. It was now truly gutted; even the front door had been torn from its hinges and carried away.

Instead of going through the house, which was now a real danger to life and limb, Terry went left, through the side gateway (it no longer had a gate) through which Chapel senior had dragged his barking dogs two years before, on the night she'd first come here looking for Rosanne and Jess. In the back yard, she circled the fast-crumbling boma and entered its open side. It now smelled hideously rank – it had clearly been used as a toilet recently – and the wooden benches around half of its interior had been ripped out, the timber used either elsewhere in another structure, or burnt for fuel or warmth.

There was evidence of many fires, both in the nominally designated fireplace and elsewhere around the boma. She was surprised to find the remains of her red candle from the previous year, burnt almost to its base.

She removed a similar red candle from her bag, along with a box of matches, and placed it next to the burnt-down stub of the old one.

She lit it, and waited while the flame flickered and found its rhythm. Watching it burn steadily, she whispered, 'Rest easy, my darling girl.'

Outside, across the muddy dirt road, the swollen river flowed implacably past.

Friday 23 July 2010

Freddie Patrizio and Ryan Chapel were on their way back to the Chapel farm in the bakkie, racing the quickly gathering dark. They had been in town, buying stuff for the braai that night – meat, beer for the boys, sweet cider for the girls, brandy, vodka, Coke and Sprite. They hadn't needed to score weed or any other party drugs – Ryan had a shitload of the stuff back at the farm. Not that he was going to be handing out any for free. Everyone paid. That was the deal. It had been making him and Annie a small fortune.

It was bucketing down – it was midwinter, one of the wettest rainy seasons on record in this part of the world – and Ryan was wondering if the weather would keep some of his friends away from the party tonight. He hoped not. He liked being the centre of attention in the boma on the farm, surrounded by a good-sized crowd. They could all smoke and drink as much as they wanted there, and do other stuff as well, away from the controlling eyes of their parents. His father was cool with it – everyone knew that.

Ryan, at the wheel, allowed himself a little grin. Annie. Things were going well there. He wasn't the kind of guy to limit himself to one chick but he might make an exception for Annie. She was very chill, very cool. He'd been a bit nervous of telling her about his drug enterprise, and showing her his stash, but she'd clocked the business sense of it immediately, and suggested she start selling to the girls in their year at school. He could handle the guys.

Then he frowned. If only she could shake Jess. It was like they were joined at the hip or something, and Jess was such a bloody nun. Ryan didn't get it, couldn't see what Annie saw in Jess, who always followed the rules and thought she was so much better than everyone else. He made Annie swear never to tell Jess about the drugs – she was just the kind of bitch to report them.

His mood souring, Ryan pressed his foot harder on the fuel pedal, pushing it almost flat to the floor. He wasn't making any allowances for the filthy weather, and the bakkie was flying along, the wheels spraying sheets of water. Occasionally it aquaplaned but this he anticipated, steering into the slide and recovering control without any problem. He had been driving farm vehicles since he was able to look over the steering wheel, so not only did he have the confidence of years of experience, he was also protected by the teenage belief that nothing bad could happen to him, that he would live forever.

As the two boys took the last long bend and headed towards the bridge, Freddie wound down the window. Bitterly cold rain-saturated air immediately flooded the cabin. '*Woo-hoo!*' Freddie yelled, sticking one hefty arm out the window, then kneeling up on the seat and pushing his large, square head out.

'Close that, you arsehole. It's cold,' Ryan shouted. He slowed briefly as the bakkie hit the bridge, then began to speed up again.

'Wait, slow down,' Freddie called, swiping a hand across his eyes to clear the rain from his vision and staring back at something the bakkie had just raced past. 'Stop! Stop!'

'I can't stop, arsehole, I'm on the bridge.'

'Okay, stop on the other side.'

'What for?'

'I just wanna do something.'

Ryan rolled his eyes but did as his friend asked, pulling the bakkie off the road on the far side of the bridge and bringing it to a halt.

Freddie, soaked down to his barrel-like upper chest, pulled his head back inside the open window and opened the passenger door.

'What you doing?' Ryan asked. 'It's pissing with rain.'

'I know. Just wait. I just wanna do something,' Freddie said again, then he jumped down, slammed the door and ran back onto the bridge.

Ryan leaned over and wound up the passenger window. Then he lit a cigarette and cracked the driver's window. Sitting back, he looked in the rear-view mirror. He could see Freddie on the bridge, hunkered over something at the side of the road.

A sudden squall sent the bakkie rocking and a heavy sheet of rain noisily blanketed the windscreen. 'Shit,' Ryan said, and hit the hooter twice, then held his hand down on the third honk.

The passenger door was flung open and Freddie, drenched and shedding rivulets of water, hurled himself back into the cab. 'Okay, go!' he yelled.

Ryan started the bakkie. 'What did you do?' he asked.

Freddie laughed maniacally, a jagged, metallic sound in the closed space of the bakkie cab. 'Ag, nothing. Just left a little surprise for someone on the bridge.'

II
SUMMER 2016

The roadworks have created a warzone-like landscape. Captain Tamara Cupido pulls the van over on a patch of new tar that can't quite be called a shoulder but which provides just enough space for the vehicle to be out of the path of the traffic rushing by. Peak hour will begin soon, and the flow is already starting to pick up.

She gets out and stands with her back against the closed driver's door, sweating in her uniform. 'Jissis, people drive like maniacs,' she says to herself, as a car goes by at such speed that it tousles her hair. She yells after it, 'Speed limit is sixty!'

The driver, either not noticing or not caring that she's from law enforcement, puts his right hand out the window and gives her the finger. Then he's gone over the next rise.

She shakes her head, then walks around the back of the van and clambers up the embankment. The roads department began this project about six years ago, working section by section on the national road between the city and the country's northern border. It's being upgraded from a simple two-lane road into a giant dual carriageway separated by a raised median.

This approximately thirty-kilometre-long section centred more or less on the turnoff to the town has been done in starts and stops, with nothing happening for months at a time, followed by frenzied activity. It's in a frenzied period now.

Cupido finds herself admiring the sheer planning the massive project requires – quite aside from the fact that the drought has meant that they can't draw from the dangerously low reservoir, and have to bring in their own recycled water in bowsers.

The road engineers have to work out how to do all the upgrades while keeping the traffic flowing, so there's got to be at least one lane open all the time. This means working on only certain stretches of either side of the old road at a time, while a stop-go system controls traffic on the single other lane remaining open for use. The old road is chopped up and the tar removed, before the loaders, asphalt mixers, rollers and graders come in to excavate, level and lay what will be just a section of one lane of the four that will ultimately make up the four-lane dual carriageway.

Looking down at the section of new tarmac girded by the raised embankment of raw red earth on which she's standing, the detective thinks to herself, So this stretch of road didn't exist just last week.

From her vantage point at the top of the slope, there's a limited view in either direction – this particular section travels through undulating countryside, and the old road dipped and swooped. The engineers are levelling out the gradient as they build the new road, she sees, so the new dual carriageway will be far less hilly than the old road.

Cupido understands the need for progress but she thinks it's a bit of a shame that they'll lose the old road. This section, on the southern side of the little town that is the centre of her region of responsibility, has lots of familiar landmarks that will be demolished or moved, and she'll miss them. Or people will pass at such speed that they just won't notice them.

She looks south, towards the city. That way, for example, although she can't see it from here, she knows there's a pan near the road. In winter it's full, and sometimes there are pelicans on it. Mad birds, she thinks; they're so big up close, it's hard to believe they can fly.

Well, she says in winter, but what she means is in normal winters. Winters in these parts haven't been normal for some years, so the pan hasn't been full for a while. She wonders where the pelicans have gone.

Then she turns and looks in the other direction – north, towards the town. From here, she can only see the tops of the copse of bluegum trees which are now on the far side of the largely disused old road. Soon, the road crew will chop up the old road, section by section, and re-tar it, and it'll finally become the two-lane northbound side of the dual carriageway.

That clump of bluegum trees was a trusted landmark on the old road, but once the dual carriageway is built, nobody will even notice it as they fly by.

Monday 22 February
4.21 p.m.

The *tick-tick* of cooling metal is the only sound for some minutes. Then, slowly, the cicadas start up again, their insistent zizzing in the superheated late afternoon increasing quickly in volume. The high-pitched shrieking has once again saturated the air, its jet-engine intensity making it sound as if the calls are coming from everywhere at once.

Most of the cicadas are in a stand of eighteen soaring bluegums, planted very close together, about forty metres from the roadworks, and down a fairly steep gradient. They are on private land.

There is absolutely no evidence of the passage of the small car off the road and into the bluegum copse. It had happened so fast, the ear-splitting sound of cracking wood and crumpling metal a giant compression shock to the surroundings, but was over almost as soon as it had begun. Branches that hadn't broken but had bent in the path of the car had sprung back, and to the casual observer the bluegum plantation looked exactly the same before as it did after the incident.

When it left the road, the car, a blue 1996 VW CitiGolf, was travelling at ninety-four kilometres per hour: thirty-four kilometres above the signposted speed limit for this stretch of the road. It was just fast enough to carry the car in a neat trajectory over the sizeable donga formed by the actions of the digger-loader that had worked on this section some months before, and into the bluegum plantation.

The little vehicle's short flight through the copse was arrested by two large tree trunks. It struck the first a glancing blow; the left bumper gouged a deep wound in the wood as the car flipped over; and then the blue Golf ploughed almost head-on into the second trunk, its windscreen cracking with a whip-like sound, its bonnet superstructure crumpling in an instant, shoving the engine backwards into the bulkhead.

There, the broken car stopped: upside down, about two metres off the ground, its roof cradled in a dense mat of interlocking bluegum branches, it rocked briefly as the last of the kinetic energy from the crash dissipated.

For a few moments, the faintly medicinal whiff of eucalyptus hangs in the air, mingling with the smell of freshly exposed wood.

Then it, too, is gone.

Up on the road, the next vehicle comes over the rise and goes past, the driver observing the speed limit, unaware of the catastrophic occurrence of just moments before.

Monday 22 February
6.44 p.m.

The first thing Imelda Uys is aware of is the deafening buzz of cicadas.

The second is the pain.

She tries to move her right arm and an agonising bolt shoots up its length. It's so sudden and violent that black spots appear in her vision and she thinks for a moment she's going to be sick. She stops moving and stays very still until the waves of pain subside.

Her mouth hurts too. And there's something wrong with her eyes – the black spots have faded but something's still obscuring her vision. Imelda blinks once, slowly, and when it doesn't hurt, she blinks rapidly, trying to clear her eyes.

She's beginning to see more clearly – but she can't make sense of what she's seeing.

She can see a car steering wheel and part of a dashboard. It's her car. Glancing down, she recognises the odometer and other dials and gauges. She can see trees – branches and leaves – through the windscreen. The windscreen is cracked. But there's something wrong with the trees: they look like trees in a child's drawing, randomly executed.

Imelda continues blinking. Slowly, she moves her eyes from left to right, trying to take in what she's seeing and make sense of it.

She can feel a line of pressure diagonally across her upper torso, above her breasts. There's an unfamiliar feeling of fullness in the top of her head.

Very slowly, and keeping it in the horizontal plane, Imelda moves her head to the left. No pain. She tries to repeat it to the right but something prevents her.

She moves her head to the left again and looks out the passenger window, noting the peculiar position of both the window and the door, which seem to be too high, or maybe too low. She gazes, concentrating hard, through the tangle of leaves and branches. What is she seeing?

She hears something: it's a deep rumbling that she can feel reverberating inside the car. The doppler effect of the noise, coming and then going, tells her that it's the sound of a very large vehicle moving past nearby.

Now that she knows that there's a road quite close to her, she can hear the hum of passing cars, and more noisy trucks.

'Help!' she tries to scream.

But the sound that emerges from her throat is a soft croak, and jissis the pain almost makes her faint.

Now she's identifying the taste in her mouth as blood, and an over-swollen feeling in her tongue tells her that she's probably bitten it.

She carefully flexes her left hand. It doesn't hurt. Slowly, she moves her left arm. No pain.

She puts her left hand up to her face and wipes her eyes, then looks at her fingers.

More blood.

Monday 22 February
7.18 p.m.

Imelda is upside down.

It's taken her a while to orientate herself, because she's in shock and pain, and can't remember anything that happened before she ended up hanging upside down in her seatbelt, in her upside-down car, in what appears to be a forest which is definitely near a road. It's hurting her head to think.

She's worked out that the blood in her eyes was running out of her mouth. It feels like she's bitten quite a big chunk out of her tongue, but the bleeding seems to have stopped now. She can see, and she can turn her head all the way to left. She can't turn her head to the right because the seatbelt is up against her ear on that side.

That full feeling in the top of her head has intensified – it feels like her skull, in the unusual position of being the part of her body closest to the ground, is filling with fluid. Imelda doesn't know if being upside down for any length of time is dangerous to her wellbeing but she does know that it doesn't feel good.

There's something seriously wrong with her right shoulder, which is an epicentre of pain. The pain radiates all the way down her right arm, and the entire right side of her torso is also throbbing and aching.

She can't feel her legs and she doesn't know what this means although she knows it's probably not good either. She can see enough by casting her eyes downwards to tell that the steering wheel and dashboard aren't in the right place – they've both shifted, and the steering wheel is lodged up against her midriff. She's actually grateful for this: it means that the seatbelt across her upper torso isn't supporting her entire weight, and therefore that it isn't cutting with too much intensity into her neck under her ear on the right side (although it's still pretty bloody eina); the steering wheel has pushed her quite firmly against the back of the driver's seat and is holding her there.

One good thing: her left arm seems unhurt. Now she's using her left hand to feel around and try to establish what's happened to the car, and if there's anything usable in reach. First prize would be her cellphone, which must be in her bag. She almost always puts her bag in the footwell on the passenger side. With luck, it will still be in the car and within reach.

Her cellphone rings.

The sound is so unexpected that it startles her, and the tiny involuntary movement of surprise she makes sets up a ricochet of agony in her shoulder that's so bad that she groans – it's an animalistic sound that she's never heard herself make before.

By the time the waves of pain have abated and she's able to think about anything else, the ringing has stopped – the call has gone to voicemail. She still doesn't know where the phone is.

There aren't many people who have her cellphone number, and even fewer who would phone her. There's her husband, Dewald, of course, but they both have busy day jobs, and tend not to call each other unless it's an emergency.

The irony of this – that if anything could be called an emergency, it's this – doesn't escape her. She breathes out slowly through her nose and squeezes her eyes shut, careful to keep her right side very still.

Her memory of the time leading up to finding herself here is fuzzy, but if she's missed a shift at either of her jobs, one of her colleagues might be calling – but it's unlikely. People miss shifts all the time for various reasons, valid or otherwise. There's a roster of people who will fill in, and usually the next person on the list is called. Very occasionally a concerned colleague may call a work friend who hasn't turned up for her shift, but she doesn't really have any work friends.

Her dad is dead, or as good as. Her mom is dead too – if not actually, then at least to her. She has no sisters or brothers. If she's got aunts and uncles, or any other extended family, she doesn't know who or where they are.

She still doesn't know where she is, but she's worked out that it's evening: although it's still very warm – hot, even – she can see the quality of the light filtering through the trees changing, and it's clear that the sun is getting low.

She thinks it's Monday evening. What she can piece together of the day is bitty and confusing, but she can clearly remember having a braai with Dewald, last night, she thinks, then going to her job at the municipality. She's pretty sure she can also remember sleeping alone in their bed last night. Dewald was working a night shift at the quarry. And she thinks she went to work at the pharmacy this morning, because she'd ordered an extra lot of antihistamine eyedrops. The heat and dust of this very dry summer has significantly increased the incidence of hayfever, and she remembers signing for them.

So it's Monday evening, she thinks to herself. And the last place she remembers being is the pharmacy, some time today. Which is all very well, she thinks, but of absolutely no help to her in solving her immediate dilemma. She contemplates the very real possibility that it's going to get dark before anyone finds her, and she's going to have to spend the night alone here, hanging upside down, in her upside-down car.

She has to free herself. She knows that moving is going to cause terrible pain in her shoulder, and she's not sure what it's going to do to her legs, but it's not like she's got a choice. It's get out of this seatbelt and out of this car and out of this forest and up to the road, or stay here, trapped, overnight.

Moving slowly to keep her shoulder as still as possible, she feels around the centre console for the seatbelt buckle. There! That was easy.

She's right-handed, and she usually pushes the tongue of the belt into the buckle with her right hand. The various bits and pieces of the seatbelt feel unfamiliar, but working carefully and methodically, she finds the release button with her left hand. She presses it and there's no resistance: it gives immediately; there's no 'click'.

She presses it again; it gives again, silently – there's no resistance whatsoever.

She closes her eyes and breathes in and out, in and out. She isn't going to panic. There must be a reason for this.

She tries to envisage exactly what the seatbelt looks like. She's put the flippen thing on and clicked it off thousands of times since she bought this car, but she's never examined it closely. She imagines the silver tongue – is it solid, or is there a hole in it? How does it clip into the buckle? What holds it? How does it work?

Frustration gets the better of her and she pushes the useless release button three, four, five times, knowing it's not going to work but at a total loss as to what else to do.

'Flip,' she says.

Monday 22 February
9.31 p.m.

It doesn't seem possible, but Imelda thinks she's been asleep. The last thing she remembers is trying to work out what the safety-belt mechanism looks like, and now it's pitch dark.

Or maybe she's been unconscious.

She stares into the darkness to her left and strains her ears. There's a dense silence – a 180-degree reversal of the ear-splitting chorus of the cicadas of earlier on. It's a totally still and apparently moonless night, because there's absolutely no movement in the trees and no light whatsoever. There's no sound from the road. She longs to hear a passing car – even if there's no way for them to know that she's here, hanging upside down in her car in this clump of trees, at least she'll know that life's going on out there.

The full feeling in the top of her skull has crept down to her eyes, which feel tight and puffy. She touches them gently with her left hand, then rubs them, trying to get off the dried blood which seems to have matted her eyelashes together.

It's still very warm, almost hot, and she's thankful for that. Being freezing would have been an additional misery she wouldn't want to have to cope with. However, the downside of a pleasantly warm night in this region, of course, is that the heat is unbearable during the day.

She considers the irony of being grateful for this hot summer night, when all she and Dewald have done for the last few months is moan about it. Summers out here in this largely rural part of the country are always hot, but this last one has been an absolute doozy – it hasn't dropped much below thirty degrees at night, which is a hot summer daytime temperature in most places, and the mosquitoes have come in relentless squadrons. It's been far too hot to sleep in nightclothes or under any bedlinen; usually, it's a case of spreading out as much as they can in their double bed, trying to avoid touching each other. They've run the small fan, standing it on the tallboy dresser and aiming it at their bed, when the heat and the sweat and the mosquitoes have become more than they can bear, but electricity is expensive.

The heat has come hand in hand with a devastating drought. In its second year now, it's wiped the colour green from the palette of the landscape, and painted everything in parched tans and desiccated beiges. The customary evening breezes, which usually bring welcome relief at the end of the blistering summer days, either don't come at all, or, if they do, they gust hot and dry. Dusty eddies rise from the shimmering fields, where farmers' wheat crops have shrivelled and died.

The river, usually a substantial waterway that irrigates many of the crops grown on its banks, and even hosts an annual canoe marathon, hasn't been this low in over twenty years, according to those in the know. The water level has dropped alarmingly over the last few months, and the flow has slowed almost to a stop. The local reservoir, which is fed by the river and serves the town's residents as well as the fairly large community living around it (including the little settlement where she and Dewald live), has also emptied to a point where the municipality has set the daily water allowance per person at eighty litres – and it's amazing how little that actually is, when everything is taken into account.

Thinking about this focuses Imelda's attention on what she knows is going to become a serious problem: she's thirsty. She comforts herself with the thought that it's not too bad yet, although she'd love to be able to rinse the metallic taste of blood out of her mouth and maybe ease the aching in her tongue.

It's okay, she tells herself. She just has to get through this night. Dewald will be looking for her …

She recalls that he wasn't there when she got home early this morning. He was working a double, she reminds herself – 9 p.m. to 9 a.m. When was his next shift? Did he say it was the same time the next night, which would be tonight – because if so, he will definitely have noticed by now that she hasn't been home and he'll be looking for her. She usually goes home between finishing work at the pharmacy at the end of the working day, and starting her night shift at the municipality.

Or did he say his shift was 3 p.m. to 3 a.m?

Or was it another time entirely?

Was he working double shifts or split shifts?

Imelda can't remember. She'd assumed that they'd connect whenever they could through the week, and that on the weekend, when they both had time off for two whole days and nights, they'd finally be able to catch up properly.

Tapping into her naturally practical side, she decides to try to think systematically of possible scenarios. It's got to be done, so she lets herself think of the worst-case one first: say Dewald is working shifts that make it possible that he won't notice her absence for a while – how long would 'a while' be? She tries to work it out, imagining possibilities for Dewald's shifts, but her head hurts and she feels a bit nauseous, and she can't get it straight in her mind.

The feeling of being completely overwhelmed and totally helpless defeats her, and she begins to cry. But this instantly increases the pressure in her head, and she feels mucus pool in the upper part of the back of her throat, beginning to run unnaturally into her sinuses.

She forces herself to stop crying. The snot isn't going to be able to fight gravity and exit through her nostrils. 'Hell, no,' she says into the darkness, her voice thick and gravelly. 'No flippen way am I drowning in my own tears.'

Tuesday 23 February
1.54 a.m.

Again, Imelda can't tell if she's been asleep or not – the darkness is so dense that it makes no difference if her eyes are open or closed.

She also doesn't know how far into the night it is. It could be hours this side of midnight, or heading for dawn. She prays it's the latter.

She hasn't heard a car or truck for ages. This makes her hope that it's the small hours, and that it won't be long before the sun rises.

The copse around her is curiously silent too. She doesn't know if it's because it's too hot for any nocturnal wildlife to be moving about much, or if the proximity of what sounds like a main road has scared off whatever animals may have at one stage made their home in these trees. Whatever the reason, she's grateful for it. She wouldn't like to be worrying about mosquitoes or creepy-crawlies of any size and description in addition to everything else.

'Everything else' includes her lungs. Something's happened to her breathing – she tries to take a deep breath but there's a pain in her chest that stops her from inflating her lungs all the way, and anyway the steering wheel is restricting her movement.

As long as she stays absolutely still, the pain in her right side is an ache. But she can't stay absolutely still – the stillness itself is causing her pain. She squeezes her eyes shut and breathes out shallowly through her nose. She mustn't panic.

Dewald is a sensible, no-nonsense person, she thinks. Even if he doesn't realise she's missing until later today, which she thinks is Tuesday, he will immediately phone around and find out where she was and where she was going, put two and two together, and come and find her.

Okay, so she can remember braaiing with Dewald at home, late Sunday arvie. She made coleslaw; he cooked boerewors and lamb ribbetjies. They had coffee afterwards. Dewald had added a shot of Amarula to his. The small bottle of Amarula cream liqueur had been a birthday present from her to him, even though they had agreed not to buy each other birthday presents and rather put the money into their savings. She had straight coffee, because she was going to work soon, and anyway she wasn't that keen on alcohol. Dewald wasn't working until 9 p.m., so he'd have plenty of time to process the booze before he went on shift.

She'd driven to the municipality on Sunday evening. She worked there as the night receptionist. The national road was, as expected on a Sunday at that time, quiet, and the drive was fairly quick and easy, despite the roadworks and numerous stop-go setups. She'd clocked in for her shift a bit before 6 p.m.

The night shift on the municipal switchboard was usually pretty uneventful. Sometimes someone might phone to report a water leak, or that their electricity had gone off. Very occasionally she got a report about a domestic disturbance, or a dog barking continuously. There was a list of referral phone numbers pinned to the wall – the police for crimes (including domestic issues) and noise complaints, the engineering division for anything to do with water or the roads, the electricity company for power failures.

Sometimes the phone didn't ring at all for the entire shift. Imelda usually took knitting or a book to keep her occupied but she remembers now that she'd forgotten to take either last night, and had ended up drawing rough sketches of their dream home on paper she'd filched from the photocopying room down the hall.

She and Dewald have talked about this imaginary home of

theirs often on and off over the six years they've been married, and now, with their five-year plan firmly in place, it feels as if it has moved ever so slightly into a space of possibility. They don't know where the house will be, or even, really, what it will look like (although she's privately formed a clear picture of it in her mind). They know only more or less how much they'll be able to afford, and how much they need to save to put down a deposit. They both know there's no guarantee they'll get a bond, but they'll cross that bridge when they come to it.

She remembers now drawing both a floor plan of the layout of the house, and a picture of the house from the front. It's a modest double-storey with a bay window on the right-hand side downstairs in the living room, which will look out onto a pretty little garden that she'd plant herself. It will have a tall tree in it, to give generous shade in the hot summers. Her and Dewald's bedroom will be upstairs, above the living room, and it will have a beautiful view over a lake or out towards a row of hills. It will have a small, clean, immaculately finished bathroom en suite. She isn't anyone's idea of an artist, so the picture wasn't accomplished in the very least, but it had made her smile.

The floor plan had also given her satisfaction: she'd included a large kitchen at the back of the house, with double glass doors leading out onto a covered verandah where she and Dewald could braai together on summer evenings. She'd put one of those little closed wood-burning fireplaces in the living room for the long, cold winters. She'd drawn an additional room upstairs – not for children (they didn't want any) or visitors (they never had any), but maybe for her sewing things and books, or Dewald's vast vinyl and CD collection.

Dewald doesn't know this, and she knows he wouldn't be happy if he found out, but she's already begun collecting things for their home. She watches out for sales and specials, and she recently bought a gorgeous pure-white pure-cotton queen-sized duvet cover, embroidered in one corner with tiny delicate yellow flowers. It's the most beautiful thing she's ever owned, and sometimes, when Dewald isn't at home, she goes out to the garage, where she's stored it carefully wrapped in brown paper, then plastic, in a large cardboard box, hidden among all the boxes of Dewald's record collection, and takes it out to look at it and run her hands over the cool, smooth fabric.

Even on special, it was expensive, but she's in charge of their current account, into which both their salaries are paid, so it's unlikely Dewald will find out. He trusts her completely to look after their money carefully – and mostly, she does, she tells herself now, tamping down the wraith of guilt that drifts into her mind. And this isn't just an indulgence for her, it's for both of them, she tells herself. And even if he did find out, she's sure he'd understand. Wouldn't he?

These are difficult thoughts, and Imelda resolves that as soon as she's out of here, she'll confess to Dewald about the duvet cover. It's not okay to keep secrets from her husband.

She feels better having made this decision, and takes further comfort in the knowledge that when Dewald finds her – because she's at least ninety percent sure that he'll be looking for her by now – he's likely to be so relieved that he won't be too annoyed about her extravagance.

Her thinking having come full circle back to the awful circumstances in which she now finds herself, she concentrates on the previous evening, continuing to try to pull together the pieces of the last twenty-four hours.

So she'd drawn pictures of their dream house, she recalls. And she'd got off shift at midnight, and gone home to sleep. And she remembers clearly that Dewald hadn't been there to snuggle up against because of the extra shifts he's working. Of course, if he had been there, the snuggling wouldn't have been for long – just until they both got so hot they couldn't bear to touch each other.

The next day, other than receiving and logging in the additional consignment of eyedrops at the pharmacy, she doesn't remember anything about what she'd done at work or anything else leading up to … what? What had happened to her?

She knows, of course, that she must have had an accident.

But if there's been an accident, why is she here alone? If she'd hit someone, or someone else had hit her, then there would be evidence up on the road, surely? The national road is always swarming with people associated with the roadworks – labourers, managers, land surveyors, drivers – so why hasn't anyone sounded the alarm? Why hasn't anyone come to find her?

Despite her dire circumstances, this is the first series of clear thoughts Imelda has had for ages, and it's almost as good as a ray of actual light.

She swallows the thickish mucus in her mouth. It's becoming worryingly difficult to swallow upside down. She's very thirsty now.

She can't stay here, trapped like this. She's going to have to make a plan as soon as it's light enough to see.

Tuesday 23 February
4.15 a.m.

She's not sure if her eyes are tricking her or not, but the quality of the light seems to be changing again, and Imelda prays that it means dawn isn't far off.

She's not doing well. She's sore all over, and that ache in her right side that not so long ago felt manageable as long as she didn't move isn't just an ache any more. It's a hot, radiating pain. Although she's pretty sure she still can't feel her legs, she can also weirdly feel pain in them, which is a contradiction she can't explain but is just the way it is. Her head is full of pounding pain – the worst headache she's ever had – and the pounding is also in her face, which feels swollen and feverish.

And flip, she's thirsty.

She's spent the last few hours – it's felt like days – trying to distract herself by remembering how she and Dewald met, and their 'whirlwind romance' (it's what they call it when they refer to it to each other – they both enjoy the silliness of it), and their marriage, and their life since. And it's worked, up to a point. But now all she can think about is how much she needs water.

She stares out of the passenger window, through the trees – searching for visible light or movement, for anything to break the terrible monotony of this endless flippen night. But all remains darkish and still.

She'd got married in a dress she'd bought at the town's secondhand – 'pre-loved' – clothes shop. It was pale blue, knee length, with cap sleeves and a sweetheart neckline – not most people's idea of a wedding dress, but she loved it.

Dewald had paid for it, although she had refused to let him see it until their wedding day. It had been on sale because it was a summer dress and she'd bought it in the middle of winter.

By some miracle the late-July day when they got married had dawned clear and had warmed up so much by early afternoon that when they had to present themselves at the magistrate's office, she hadn't even had to use the woolly cardigan she'd bought to go with it.

Dewald had worn jeans and a smart shirt, pale yellow. He had looked so handsome.

They had put a picnic together – just egg-mayo sandwiches and a bottle of sparkling wine, and some crisp green apples – and driven to the river, where they'd had their 'reception'. The river back then was overfull. It had broken its banks already once that winter and drowned the vineyards alongside. The water was fast-moving and noisy.

Dewald had used the wine to toast her: 'To the bride.'

'To the groom,' she'd countered with a smile.

They were a perfect family of two. Imelda had never believed in love at first sight, or that there was only one special someone out there for each person on earth. It just seemed so completely unlikely that out of seven billion people, there was one made exactly for her. But it turned out there really was, and that he'd found her. They'd found each other.

Even now, hanging upside down in her crashed car, with pain in every part of her body and her tongue grotesquely swollen from injury and lack of water, she gives a tiny grin: she can hardly believe how lucky she's been.

They had only known each other for two weeks when they got married but it had felt, right from the start, as if they'd known each other forever – from other lives, maybe. She felt that Dewald got her on a level she'd never experienced before, and she knew that he felt the same. He told her often enough.

They'd had the 'children or no children' talk early on. It

had, in fact, been among their first conversations, as if they'd both known by some sort of instinct that it was an important subject to address. Neither wanted children. Neither had had a happy time growing up; both had had parents who had at best disappointed them and at worst made their lives a misery. They had no wish to either revisit this with their own offspring, even if not intentionally, or to try to correct the wrongs of the past by doing it over again.

'Just you and me,' Dewald had said, holding Imelda tightly in his arms on their wedding night. With perfect timing, the rain had started again in the early evening, and by the time they'd got into bed, it was bucketing down outside. Their little home was a warm cocoon, their double bed a nest.

'Just you and me,' she tries to whisper to herself, remembering, but her throat is too dry to produce recognisable sounds.

Tuesday 23 February
5.13 a.m.

Thank goodness for daylight.

Imelda has watched the foliage around her change colour as the sun began rising, and now the low morning rays are streaming through the trees in places, bringing blessed light.

On a less cheerful note, it's been warm all night and Imelda can already feel eddies of heat curling into the upside-down car. It's going to be another scorcher of a day.

'Today I get out of here,' she tries to say, intending to give herself courage by this hopeful statement, but her efforts produce only a soft grating sound, and she immediately and bitterly regrets the movement of her tongue, which is unbelievably sore.

She's feeling terrible from top to bottom (or, given her circumstances, bottom to top) – lightheaded, which seems totally contradictory, as hanging upside down for all this time has made it feel as if the blood has pooled and coagulated in the top of her skull. She has no idea what the biological consequences might be of her unusual position but the mere idea of her blood not circulating back out of her brain is making her feel despairing.

And breathing has become even more difficult – she's given up trying to fill her lungs, and the shallow panting she's been reduced to has made her feel panicky.

There's no moisture at all in her mouth now so it's pointless trying to lick her lips, which feel tight and swollen. It goes without saying that she's horribly thirsty, and she realises that she's hungry too.

Whatever is broken in her shoulder seems to have settled as a result of her care to not move. She flexes her left hand, then slowly bends it up and down from the elbow – it's fine, she can do this without moving her right side at all.

The phantom pains in her legs have abated; they were replaced for some time last night by uncomfortable pins-and-needles, but now they're just numb.

Her hearing is, apparently, unaffected – probably the only thing in her body that's working properly. She can hear traffic on the road nearby, which started about an hour ago (she estimates) and has been picking up steadily. And there's something else – there's not only passing traffic, there's also something going on, obviously associated with the roadworks, in one area that can't be too far from her: she can hear the sounds of heavy vehicles arriving and leaving, and of what could be hydraulic equipment.

What she hasn't heard, and it's worrying, is her cellphone ringing again after that one call last night. Surely by now Dewald has realised she's missing and has tried to phone her? Or one of her jobs – she may not know what exactly happened to her yesterday, but she knows that last night, at least, she missed a shift at the municipality.

She tries to remember how much charge her cellphone had the last time she looked at it, but she uses it so seldom that she just doesn't know. She's not efficient at keeping it charged, which is something Dewald has been on at her about.

He nags her about so little. She loves him so much.

Her life before Dewald was a long and mainly miserable saga of alternately trying to survive and treading water. Growing up, for her, had involved mainly keeping out of the way of her increasingly resentful and neglectful mother, who solved her own myriad problems by trying to drink reality away. She'd never met her father; her mother had told her he was dead, and while her mother had never given her any reason to believe her about anything, Imelda also had no desire to track down an absent parent who hadn't cared enough about her to stick around.

At 16, she'd left school and got a job as a cashier at a local supermarket, and saved enough money to put down a month's security deposit. She had moved into a tiny one-room flat on the outskirts of the town, which she shared with Xoliswa, a 17-year-old with a tiny baby, Themba, who slept curled into his mother's tummy.

The flat had come 'fully furnished' with two single beds, a very small table with two chairs, and a 'kitchenette' (a counter with a kettle, a toaster and a griller on it), with a miniature sink, cold water only, in one corner. The communal showers (two, both filthy) and toilets (four, ditto) were downstairs, at the end of a long cement corridor that smelled of mould.

Her mind jumps to the day she met Dewald, outside the municipal offices. She can't remember why she'd gone there – to pay some utility account, probably – but she can remember Dewald's exact expression as he came up to her, standing on her own waiting for the doors to reopen after lunch, and asked her, 'Are you the queue?'

She can see his face in her mind's eye: his slightly raggedy eyebrows over warm, gentle, green eyes; his perfectly ordinary nose; his mouth with its big bottom lip.

In her mind, a halo of golden light suddenly shines around his head as her overheated, blood-saturated brain begins short-circuiting.

'Hi,' he says to her. 'You're so beautiful. Please be my wife.'

She smiles at him, and golden rays shoot out of her eyes and hearts fly around her like Disney birds.

He takes her in his arms and orchestral music swells as he lowers his mouth to hers …

Tuesday 23 February
10.07 a.m.

Imelda smiles at Dewald across the table. It's set with pristine white napery, and the silvery cutlery sparkles. She lifts her glass of red wine and says, 'To us!'

Dewald, looking dashing in a tuxedo (and, curiously, wearing a dapper little moustache), raises his glass and toasts her. 'You look beautiful, my darling,' he says.

And she does. She's wearing a deep-red velvet dress with a tight-fitting bodice and a full skirt (even though she's sitting down, she just knows this), and the kind of high heels that usually make her totter (but she knows that she will walk in these with perfect elegance), and she has on tiny diamond earrings. Her long hair is done up on top of her head in a simple, elegant arrangement that shows off her pretty neck.

She smiles, showing her straight white teeth, and bats her long eyelashes.

They're in a very fancy restaurant that might be in Paris – she's sure that if she looks left, out the huge picture window she knows is on the far side of the room, she'll see the Eiffel Tower.

'Are you warm enough, my darling?' Dewald asks her. 'Enjoying the fire?'

Their table is indeed right next to a roaring log fire, built in a fireplace that's about the size of their little bedroom back home.

'I'm fine,' she says, delicately wiping a bead of sweat from her top lip. 'In fact, I'm a little warm.'

'I've asked the maitre d' to move us but he says there are no other seats in the restaurant,' Dewald tells her. 'I'm afraid we'll have to just make do.'

'But Dewald, I'm cooking,' Imelda says. She can now feel the sweat pouring down behind her ears and between her breasts.

'We *have* to move, please!'

Before her horrified eyes, Dewald begins melting, his spruce moustache oozing down his face and his flesh following.

Imelda gasps as she wakes up, disoriented and feverish.

She's gigantically relieved to be out of the ghastly nightmare of watching her husband disintegrate but the reality is hardly better: it's hellishly hot already, and she judges by the quality of the light that it's still some time in the morning. Her head is pounding. Her tongue is now so swollen that it feels as if it's poking through her lips, which themselves feel like they're full of paper-cuts. The pain in her shoulder has concentrated its agony in one spot, which she thinks may be the shoulder blade that the seatbelt is cutting into.

She can still faintly hear vehicles – both passing and working – and there's an added sound which is making it hard for her to concentrate: the cicadas have started up, first one, then two, then a bunch. And now the zizzing sound is so loud that it feels physically painful. It's coming from all directions at once, and it's reverberating with such power that it also feels as if it's inside her.

Tuesday 23 February
2.12 p.m.

The heat is absolutely unbearable. It's worse than the hunger and the thirst and even the pain. And the crazy zizzing of the cicadas seems, in Imelda's mind, to be the aural version of that heat, seeping into her every pore.

The sun is high in the sky, and the only thing that's stopping the little car turning into a furnace is its position low down in the copse – the foliage of the tall trees above it filters out most of the sun's direct rays – and the fact that the windows are slightly open. The ambient temperature is, nonetheless, rising fast to fiery levels.

She's grateful now that her little car doesn't have airconditioning – it if had, the windows would've been closed and she'd be baking alive in what would effectively be a sealed metal box.

The little blue 1996 VW CitiGolf had made a significant dent in her and Dewald's savings, but they'd reckoned it was worth it. To start with, when Imelda had just the one job at the pharmacy and Dewald was working normal day shifts at the quarry, he'd taken her to work on his way to the quarry every morning, and fetched her from work every day after his shift, in his trusty old bakkie.

Then they'd come up with their five-year plan, which involved working their bums off and saving every single cent they could, so that they could put down a deposit on a house of their own. Imelda had been lucky enough to get a second job – answering the night phones at the municipality. Although Dewald insisted he didn't mind acting taxi and doing lots of extra driving – including in the middle of the night – to get his wife to her various jobs on time, after some discussion, they'd decided they had to buy her a car of her own.

They'd bought it secondhand, privately from someone who'd advertised it in the local knock-and-drop newspaper, and paid cash straight out of their savings account. This way, they hadn't had to get a loan, and had avoided having to pay interest. While initially it had felt like a huge chunk of their carefully stashed money had, distressingly, suddenly gone, Dewald pointed out that, over time, they would actually save themselves thousands by not paying interest.

The car was very basic – 'just a steering wheel and four tyres', as Dewald described it – but Imelda had quickly come to love it. She'd had to get her licence first, of course, and Dewald had helped her with that, patiently giving her driving lessons every weekend for a while, then (after she'd written and passed her learner's) handing over control of the vehicle to her on their trips together between home and pharmacy, pharmacy and municipality, municipality and home.

Imelda remembers the nerve-racking day she'd gone to do her driver's licence and passed, and Dewald's pride and delight in her. Then the incredible moment she had got into her very own car, and driven to work, a fully licensed driver, on her own for the very first time.

The fact that Imelda had her own car, and that as a consequence Dewald wasn't limited to day shifts at the quarry by her various work times, had enabled him to take on additional shifts too, and the extra money had quickly begun replenishing their savings account.

If I could just open the windows a little more, Imelda thinks, not only would the throughflow of air perhaps improve a little, but maybe I would be able to attract some attention.

She can't reach either of the window winding handles with her left hand. In desperation, she attempts to move her right hand to try to find the handle on the driver's door, and it sets up such a tidal wave of pain down her right side that she immediately has to abandon the plan. It takes what feels like forever for the waves of agony to subside.

The heat is fast becoming unendurable. She doesn't know how hot it must be for a human being to die of hyperthermia, but she thinks that the temperature inside the car must be close.

The insufferable heat and the intolerable noise of the cicadas have swamped every other thought in her head — there's simply no space for anything else. It's just filled with heat and noise.

She's been drifting in and out of consciousness for a while, and now she prays that she'll pass out again. Or die. Anything to escape this very real hell.

Wednesday 24 February
7.56 a.m.

Dewald Uys just wants to get home.

He's worked three night shifts in a row, and it's thoroughly messed with his sleeping patterns. He has that scratchy-eyed, slightly stoned feeling that comes with chronic undersleeping, and he's as hungry as a horse. Right now, what he needs most are food and sleep.

He hasn't seen Imelda, his wife, for a couple of days. At the moment she's got two jobs: she's a cashier at a pharmacy in the town from 8.30 a.m. to 4 p.m., then she takes the first shift on the emergency switchboard at the municipality from 6 p.m. to midnight. She comes home to grab some sleep, before the cycle starts again.

Usually, Dewald works 9 to 5 at the quarry, supervising the gravel pits. Normally, he would wake up early, before Imelda, and put on the coffee. Then he and his wife would have a quick breakfast together before they each started their day. But the giant upgrade on the national road has put huge additional requirements on the quarry, and Dewald is working extra shifts now, too. Not that he's complaining: he and Imelda are only too happy for the extra money.

He pulls into the gravel driveway, the stones crunching loudly under the wheels of the vehicle, and the bakkie gives a loud backfire before shuddering, apparently unwillingly, to a stop. Dewald winces. It's needed a service for months but it's one of the many things that will have to wait.

'Imelda?' he calls as he unlocks the front door and pushes it open.

A very large black dog, mostly alsation in appearance, but with one oversized ear pricked up and the other permanently flopped over, sits directly inside the front door. Her body quivers with delight at Dewald's arrival, and her long tail alternately sweeps and thumps the floor. She's wearing a very broad smile which, combined with the steady gaze of her brown wolf-like eyes, gives her a slightly crazed appearance.

'Vumba.' Dewald says her name, dropping to his knees to put his arms around the dog's neck. He buries his nose in her soft, long hair and breathes in her clean-dog smell, rubbing the top of her head with one hand. 'Where's your ma?'

Although Mel usually leaves for work around 8 a.m., he'd hoped he would get home in time to see her, even if only in passing.

He leans back on his heels and listens. The silence of the house is absolute. Tomb-like. He's missed her, he realises, and quietly clicks his tongue in disappointment.

Then he realises there's something else missing too: any residual smell of coffee or toast, early-morning constants in their kitchen. It's a subtle absence, and it may not mean anything – maybe Mel just had breakfast early – but it makes Dewald frown.

'Imelda?' he calls again, not expecting a response. Then he checks the house, Vumba padding around behind him. It doesn't take long. There are only three rooms.

In their tiny bedroom, the bed is neatly made, the way he left it yesterday afternoon – and, now that he comes to think of it, on Monday afternoon too. But because his and Imelda's non-working hours haven't been overlapping, he'd just assumed that she'd made the bed too, after getting out of it. Now he looks more closely: he can see the uppermost pillow on his side still has the dent of his head in it – his pillows haven't been fluffed up, which is something Imelda likes to do and he just can't be bothered with.

A worm of unease wriggles in his belly.

The little bathroom, too, is neat. Both he and Imelda like things tidy. But again, it's neat *his* way, not hers. The bristles of their toothbrushes, standing upright in a squat, heavy glass, are touching. Imelda always makes sure they're separated. And the bath sheets aren't folded once and hung military-style on the towel rack, with their edges perfectly squared up. They're just slung over, the way he does it.

He doesn't have to closely examine the kitchen-slash-living area with its cleared and wiped surfaces and two small chairs pushed in at the breakfast nook. He knows there'll be crumbs under the toaster (something he always leaves but Imelda never does) and that the stainless-steel sink will bear signs of suds (him) rather than having been meticulously wiped out with a dry cloth (her).

Vumba's food and water bowl are both empty although that alone doesn't really mean anything. Remarkably unflappable in all other aspects, the dog seems to be permanently starving. She can gulp down a big bowl of dog pellets in a matter of seconds. And in the heat of the drought, it's a fulltime job to keep her water bowl filled.

Dewald feeds Vumba – she falls on her bowl as if she hasn't seen food in years – and tops up her water bowl, then stands at the kitchen sink and stares out the window into the small back yard. Listening to Vumba practically inhale her pellets, he thinks to himself, When did I last speak to Mel? He rubs his face briskly with both hands and tries to recall. His hunger and exhaustion, and now a stomach-writhing anxiety, make it difficult to remember.

Sunday. It was late Sunday afternoon, before Imelda's switchboard shift. They'd had a braai. He'd cooked lamb ribs and boerewors. She'd made a coleslaw with raisins in it, the way he liked it. They hadn't talked about their hectic week ahead:

they'd both known it would be days before they'd connect again, and talking about it wouldn't help.

Today is Wednesday. He looks at his watch again: 8.20 a.m.

He opens the flap of his satchel, which he'd thrown down on the little table in the breakfast nook as he'd come into the house, and takes out his cellphone. It's on, but the battery is down to three percent. While he's looking at the screen, it goes blank and the phone dies.

He goes into the bedroom and looks in his bedside drawer, then Imelda's, for the charger. They share one and it's usually in one of the drawers. But today it's not there, and he remembers, with a burst of anxiety that actually churns his gut, that Imelda had forgotten to charge her phone, and had taken the charger with her to work on Sunday evening, intending to do it at the municipality.

'Flip,' Dewald says.

Wednesday 24 February
9 a.m.

The electronics shop in the town is just opening, and they've got a charger for him. Dewald forks out the money for it, for once not caring about the expense.

He drives straight back home, but the return trip, like the outgoing one, isn't quick, and a couple of times he thumps his fist in frustration on the steering wheel as he's held up at the various stop-go arrangements, and at the more convoluted, slower sections of the roadworks. Vumba sits happily in the passenger seat, her long black nose thrust out the window.

The gravel crunches under the bakkie's wheels as Dewald slams on the brakes in the driveway, and he leaps out of the vehicle without a thought to the over-running engine that usually bothers him so much. Vumba jumps down behind him.

In the kitchen, he plugs in his phone.

He looks at his watch: 9.35 a.m.

The cellphone takes about a minute to bank enough charge to switch on, then Dewald immediately phones Imelda's cell.

There are a couple of electronic-sounding clicks – no ringing – then he hears his wife's voice: 'Hi, it's Imelda. Please leave a message and I'll get back to you.'

'It's me. Where are you? It looks like you haven't been home. Call me,' says Dewald. His voice sounds panicky even to his own ears, and he hopes it doesn't freak Imelda out when she gets the message.

Leaving his phone on charge, Dewald scoops two spoons of coffee into the plunger. Coffee made with pre-ground beans is the single luxury in the Uyses' pantry. Imelda had at first been irritated about Dewald's insistence on buying this coffee, and one of the few arguments they'd had about money was about it, but he'd refused to give in. 'We don't drink – well, you don't drink at all and I barely drink – and we don't smoke, and we don't jol,' he'd pointed out. 'We've got to have one luxury.'

'Why can't it be an *instant* luxury, then?' Imelda had countered. 'Why must it be this expensive stuff?' But she hadn't argued with much zeal: Dewald had made a significant personal sacrifice when it came to their five-year saving plan, and no longer spent any money at all on the records and CDs that were his passionate hobby.

His collection was already vast, as was his knowledge about everything to do with popular music, from history and artists to studios and genres. But Imelda knew he would have loved to continue scouring charity and secondhand shops for the rare and amazing finds he was so good at winkling out, and doing deals with other collectors he connected with through the local knock-and-drop. He had even offered to sell his collection, the many, many boxes of which almost filled the single garage that was attached to their little rented house, and put the proceeds into their savings account, but Imelda had drawn the line at that. Their dream of owning their own house was very important, she'd said, but she didn't want Dewald to end up resenting what it had cost them.

And anyway, Imelda's more hooked than he is on the luxury coffee now: she says it's the thought of that first strong, aromatic cup in the morning that gets her out of bed, even when she's so tired that she feels she could sleep for a week.

Dewald adds the almost-boiling water and gives the mixture a stir, then positions the plunger lid on top.

He phones Imelda's cell again. Straight to voicemail.

'Flip, Mel. Where are you?'

He doesn't disconnect immediately, but takes the phone away from his ear and stares at Imelda's name on the screen.

Then he disconnects.

Vumba, stretched out at the open back door, lifts her head and looks at him, then sighs and lets her head drop again.

Dewald slowly plunges the coffee and pours himself a cup.

He phones Imelda's cell again. Straight to voicemail.

This time he doesn't leave a message.

Dewald sits at the little breakfast nook table and picks at the linoleum where it's come loose on the corner, slowly sipping his coffee. His brain is whirring.

First, is he right that Imelda hasn't been home? He knows he is, but he goes back into the bedroom anyway, and stares at the neatly made bed. Yes, Imelda's pillows are as she likes them and his aren't. It seems a very insignificant clue but he knows his wife well, and those pillows are telling him something.

'But what if she was just in a hurry, and didn't fluff up my pillows like she usually does?' he says to Vumba, who cocks her head to the side, apparently listening carefully.

He gets a sudden idea and quickly goes into the bathroom, where he peers into the grey plastic laundry basket, then leans down and picks up the top few items. 'Ja,' he says to himself. The only dirty clothes that have been added to the basket since Sunday are his.

He returns to the little living area and sits back down at the table. He's so very worried about his wife but he's trying to sort through and manage warring emotions. He wants to report his wife's disappearance to the police, but he doesn't want to draw unnecessary attention to them. What if he gets other people involved, and then Imelda turns up? She'll be so embarrassed.

He rubs his face again with both hands, feeling the callouses on the cushions at the base of his fingers scrape lightly over his skin. He doesn't know what to do. Vumba, sensing his unease, pads over and lays her big black head on his thigh. He holds out a hand and she licks it.

He and Imelda will have been married for six years this coming July, and in that time they've become a tight unit, to the exclusion of almost the entire rest of the world. Unless Imelda is an unbelievably good actress, for her, like for him, it was love at first sight.

In the course of a short conversation, held shyly outside the municipal offices in the centre of town, while they both waited for the doors to re-open after the lunch break, they'd discovered that neither of them had any family. When Imelda had asked if Dewald's parents lived in the area, he'd said, 'Oh. No. They're dead.'

Imelda had laughed spontaneously and said, 'I'm glad that you didn't say they've passed away. I hate that euphemism. My parents are dead too. And I don't have any family.'

'Me neither.'

They'd looked at each other then, and a surge of recognition – an entirely new experience for Dewald when it came to people, and women in particular – seemed to pass between them. And just like that, both their lives were suddenly profoundly changed.

Two weeks later they'd got married. Their witnesses were a draughting student doing an internship at the municipality and a cleaner.

Dewald calls Imelda's cellphone again, and once again it goes to voicemail. He looks at his watch: 9.56 a.m. He has to make some sort of decision.

He'll wait until noon, he tells himself, then he'll go to the police.

Wednesday 24 February
10.37 a.m.

The sound of the cicadas is deafening. It does indeed seem to be an exact acoustic representation of the sizzling heat.

Inside the little car, lodged tightly in its hammock of bluegum branches, upside down and about two metres off the ground, its nose crushed up against a trunk, the temperature is rising fast. Soon it will be in the forties. The only thing standing between death by overheating and the body hanging upside down in the driver's seat are many layers, reaching up many metres, of branches and foliage that filter out the direct sunlight, and the tiny respite offered by the almost imperceptible flow of air in and out of the slightly open front windows.

The body is wedged tightly against the back of the driver's seat by the stoved-in front console and steering wheel. It shows no signs of life. The face is a livid purple, the eyes swollen shut, with flecks of dried blood giving it a mottled rotten-meat look.

The collar bone is fractured, as is the bone in the upper right arm. Three of the fingers on the right hand are broken.

The legs, in the driver's footwell, in the unnatural position above rather than below the body's torso, are both crushed. There are too many broken bones to count. But, perhaps mercifully, a vital bundle of nerves at the base of the spinal column has been compressed, cutting off all messages of feeling between the destroyed limbs and the brain.

Inside the body's torso, the weight of the liver and intestines, usually safely located beneath the lungs, but now resting on them, are slowly squashing those delicate organs.

The body's heart, too, is battling. Normally, when it pumps blood down to the feet, gravity helps take it on its way. And when it pumps blood up to the head, it pumps a little harder. Now, the heart is struggling with all the extra blood that's coming at it, and fluid is beginning to leak out of the vessels.

As if the body doesn't have enough to cope with, it hasn't had any hydration for about forty hours. Between this deprivation and the body's dangerously elevated core temperature in the astonishingly hot car, it is taking a terrible battering.

Weirdly, however, the body's lack of water is going some way to alleviating the horrendous symptoms it's beginning to experience as a result of hanging upside down for a day and a half. As its fluid levels drop, liquid is being diverted to fill vital organs with blood, somewhat limiting the leakage from the vessels due to the malfunctioning blood pressure.

Wednesday 24 February
10.37 a.m.

Dewald knows it's going to go to voicemail but for about half an hour he phones Imelda's cellphone repeatedly. It's a reaction to feeling completely helpless.

Then: 'No,' he says to himself, and puts his cellphone down. He needs to think.

Imelda's night job is at the municipal offices in the town. The town is twenty-eight kilometres away. They live in a small rural community of maybe fifteen houses, just off the national road, so the drive to the town is along the national road. This previously single-lane-each-way road has been undergoing roadworks for some years now, so what at one stage was a quick, easy, relatively safe, fifteen- to twenty-minute drive between home and town now often takes considerably longer. Depending on what time of the day it is, it can be fraught with peril. Impatient drivers tailgate relentlessly, unskilled drivers speed on sections where a wrong move could easily cause a serious accident, and inexperienced drivers overtake in unsafe circumstances.

But Sunday nights are usually trouble free, with not much traffic on the road.

Dewald clicks his fingers. 'Should have done this first!' he mutters to himself, irritably.

Vumba, assuming the finger-click is for her, barks once, then realises that her owner isn't paying her any attention. She sits and lifts a paw.

Ignoring her, Dewald snatches up his cellphone and dials the municipality. The phone is answered promptly, as always.

'I'm Dewald Uys, and I'm phoning to find out if my wife, Imelda, came to work on Sunday night,' he blurts out.

There's a short pause while the woman on the other end of the line assimilates his query and decides how to deal with it. Then she says, 'Hold on, please.' There's a click followed by recorded music. Bizarrely, it's the Beach Boys singing 'Santa's Got an Airplane'.

Dewald sits in the breakfast nook, quite still but for the movement of his jaws as he nibbles nervously at the insides of his cheeks, a habit he's had since he was a child.

The Beach Boys sing tinnily into his ear for about thirty seconds ('Loop-de-loop, flip-flop, Santa's got an airplane ...'), which feels like thirty years to Dewald, then there's another click and a man's voice, overloud, says, 'Mr Uys! How can I help you?'

There's a superior smugness in the man's tone that instantly gets Dewald's back up. 'Who are you?' he asks, not intending the question to come out sounding quite so rude.

'Robertson, HR,' the man snaps back. Dewald has offended him.

'Mr Robertson,' Dewald says, trying to claw back some goodwill, 'my wife Imelda works night shift on reception. She was on duty on Sunday night, and I just wanted to know if she came to work.'

'It's Wednesday, Mr Uys,' Robertson says, unnecessarily slowly.

'I know,' Dewald replies, suppressing the urge to scream at this time-wasting moron. He's not good with words, and words are now very important. 'I've been working split shifts and night shifts, so we haven't been in touch since Sunday night. I only realised this morning that she may not have been home.'

'You two have a fight?'

The question is so inappropriately personal, the tone so arrogant, that Dewald clenches his free fist. 'No,' he replies shortly. 'Mr Robertson, I think something's happened to my wife. Please can you tell me if she was at work on Sunday night.'

'You been to the police?'

Jissis. Dewald squeezes his eyes shut. 'I'm going. I'm going now, the minute I finish talking to you. Please: was she at work on Sunday night?'

There's a small pause, filled with loathing. 'I'll check the register,' Robertson says, then there's a click and the recorded music comes on again. This time it's Dean Martin crooning 'Angel Baby'.

As Dewald sits and waits, listening to Mr Martin singing about his angel baby flipping his crazy heart right over, he works out what he's going to do next. If Imelda was at work at the municipality on Sunday night, then the next thing to find out is if she went to work at the pharmacy on Monday morning. Her shift there begins at 8.30 a.m. If she wasn't at work on Sunday night, then he has to try to figure out where she went after she left their home.

The seconds drag by. Dewald obsessively nibbles the inside of his cheeks, inadvertently drawing blood. The music, which, despite having a somewhat calming rhythm, only succeeds in creating a little tornado in his mind, and he concentrates on not thinking murderous thoughts about Dean Martin and Mr Roberts, and on staying calm. It's vital that he get this information from this awful HR man, so he's got to stay on the line and he's got to keep his temper in check.

He looks at his watch. 10.43 a.m.

He sits, eyes shut, counting slowly. He counts to a hundred and twenty.

He opens his eyes and looks at his watch: 10.46 a.m.

Jissis. Where the fuck … the flip is this register, on the flippen moon?

'*Hello?*' he screams suddenly into the phone. '*Hello?*' Then he snatches the phone away from his ear and pushes it into his midriff, stares up at the ceiling and screams, '*Fuuuuck!*'

Vumba barks twice. Dewald's anxiety is beginning to get to her.

'Sorry, girl,' he tells her. 'Shh.' Then he puts the phone to his ear again, to finally hear a click and Robertson's voice.

'She signed in at 5.45 p.m. and signed out at 12.02 a.m.' he says. The HR man's cool and exceedingly businesslike tone makes it abundantly clear that he's providing this information very much against his will.

'Thanks,' Dewald says, and is about to disconnect when Robertson adds, 'But she didn't come in on Monday night or last night.'

Dewald is momentarily thrown. He hasn't thought through the timeline that far, and he has to consider what this new bit of information means.

Robertson fills the silence, and his tone is accusatory. 'One of my staff phoned her on Monday night to find out why she wasn't there but there was no reply,' he says. 'We can't afford these kinds of no-shows, Mr Uys, so we've replaced her on the register with someone else for that shift. She needs to know that she can't …'

Dewald disconnects the call and immediately phones the pharmacy. Hopefully, this call will be easier. Unlike at the fairly large and plentifully staffed municipality, he knows most of the permanent workers at the pharmacy, by name at least, from Imelda's stories about them. Her immediate supervisor is Yolande February, and that's who he asks for when the phone is answered on the second ring.

He hears the phone being put aside, and the busy background noise of the pharmacy in full daily business swing. And he hears a voice shout, 'Yolande! Phone for you!'

Very soon, a warm female voice says, 'Yolande February. How may I help you?'

The difference in tone from the obnoxious Robertson almost brings Dewald to tears, and in fact his voice breaks a little as he explains the situation to Ms February.

'Well, she came in on Monday, Mr Uys,' Yolande says, 'but she wasn't here yesterday, and she's not in today. I meant to phone her yesterday but it's been hectic here and I have to admit I just forgot.'

'Did she seem okay on Monday?' Dewald asks. He's horrified by and ashamed of the high-pitched begging tone of his voice but he's so completely lost in fear and bewilderment that he can't do anything about it.

Ms February seems to understand. She says, 'Imelda keeps to herself, Mr Uys, but she seemed fine. I don't think she'd confide in me, or in anyone else here either, if she had a problem. She's a very private person, as you no doubt know. But there was no sign that anything was wrong.'

'Did she leave at the usual time?'

'Yes, 4 p.m.'

'Did she say where she was going?'

'No. I know she works at the municipality – have you tried there?'

'Yes, but her shift there only starts at 6 p.m. so she usually comes home first,' Dewald says. He realises that explaining this to Yolande isn't going to get him any answers but it's almost as if it's helping him clarify things in his own mind.

'Have you been to the police?'

'No. I'm going there now,' he says.

'Ja, that's probably best,' says the kindly Ms February. 'Please call if I can do anything to help.'

Wednesday 24 February
11.17 a.m.

Dewald steers his bakkie into the cobble-paved police-station parking area. They're obviously having a slow day. There are only three vehicles in the parking lot, and he gets a spot right outside the front door.

Inside, three people are on duty – one man, sitting at a desk in the back, filling in forms, and two women, both sitting at the short bank of counters in the front.

Dewald walks straight up to the first woman and says, 'I want to report a missing person.' It's a ridiculously theatrical statement. He's seen almost this exact scene on TV and in movies several times before. It strikes him as sounding, stupidly, like he's acting.

The police officer seems to think the same. 'Who is it?' she asks listlessly. Although she doesn't quite study her fingernails, she somehow gives the impression that this is what she wants to do. She doesn't bother lifting her head, but simply slides her eyes to glance up at him.

'My wife. She's been gone for two days,' he says.

The officer does now move her head. She looks at the second female officer, to her right, who's staring at him with a curious expression on her face – her eyes are slightly narrowed, as if she's sizing him up. She crooks a finger and beckons at him.

He steps sideways to her counter, relieved not to have to deal any further with the infuriating indifference of the first officer, and says, 'Do I have to fill in forms or what? My wife didn't come home on Monday night after work.'

'Take a seat,' the officer says. 'I'm Captain Cupido. I'll take your statement.'

Dewald sits.

The police officer – the captain – pulls a sheaf of paper out

161

from under the desk and holds it upright, banging it on the counter to straighten it, then carefully places it in front of her. She takes a pen from her pocket and clicks it once, twice, three times. She holds out a hand. 'ID?' she asks.

'Flip,' Dewald says, automatically patting his pockets. 'I didn't bring it.'

The detective ignores this and asks, 'Name and ID number?'

Dewald rattles these off, watching her write them down. She writes fast and clearly – Dewald is grateful for both her speed and her penmanship. They make him feel as if she knows what she's doing.

'Wife's name and ID number?'

Dewald gives her these too, and the usual list of other bits and pieces that identify human beings: place of residence, how long they've lived there, marital status, profession, how long they've been employed and by whom …

'Next of kin?' the detective asks, pen poised.

Dewald hesitates, then answers, 'Each other.'

Detective Cupido clicks her pen and looks up at him. 'No mom or dad? Either of you?'

'No,' he replies.

'Siblings? Grandparents? Aunts or uncles?'

Dewald shakes his head.

The detective shrugs and writes something.

'When last did you see ….' she refers to a place higher up on the sheet of paper '… Imelda?' she asks.

'Sunday, about 5.30 p.m. We had a braai, then she left for work.'

'How?'

'Excuse me?'

'How did she leave? Did she drive?'

'Oh, ja. She drove. A Golf. 1996. Blue.'

Detective Cupido writes this down, then looks up at Dewald and waits.

'So I got home this morning and realised that she hadn't been home.' Dewald looks pained and says, 'I didn't know for how long at first. I checked the pillows. She fluffs them, and they weren't fluffed.'

Cupido listens, her impassive face giving nothing away.

'And the toothbrushes – they were touching. And she's better about cleaning up in the kitchen,' he says. There's a moment of silence while Cupido stares, expressionless, at Dewald, and Dewald looks back. Then he suddenly gains a little confidence and adds, 'I also checked the laundry basket. No clothes since Sunday. None of hers, I mean.'

Cupido nods. 'And how do you know what was in the laundry basket on Sunday?'

'We do the laundry on Sunday mornings,' he says. 'I help because of the water restrictions. We've got an old top-loader, and it rinses out into a bin so we can use the water to flush the toilet during the week. Because of the drought, you know.'

Cupido does indeed know. The water restrictions have been a great leveller – eighty litres is a surprisingly hard ceiling to stay under when you've always been used to just switching on the tap and using the water that gushed out, apparently infinitely, but for the poorer members of the community it's required a far lesser degree of adaption. Very few of the folk who live in Captain Cupido's community even own washing machines – top-loaders or otherwise, she thinks wryly. For most of them, doing laundry means dragging the old tin tub into the back yard, filling it bucket by bucket with cold water, then manually scrub-a-dub-dubbing.

'The only things that were in the laundry basket were some of my things,' Dewald says, breaking into the detective's thoughts.

Cupido refocuses, writes for a moment or two, then looks up. 'What did you do next?' she asks.

'I tried calling her cellphone. But my phone was dead and I had to come into town to buy a charger first, because she's got our charger. We share it.'

'So you've been to town this morning already? You should have popped in,' she says.

Dewald looks for signs that she's joking but she's completely poker-faced. 'I didn't know then that she was missing,' he says. 'I didn't think …' He stops and looks down at his hands. 'I didn't know what to think.'

'Okay,' Captain Cupido says, agreeably. 'So you came into town and bought a charger and then drove all the way home again, and charged your phone.'

Dewald nods.

'And then?'

'When I phoned her, it went straight to voicemail. I've called her phone a lot this morning. Voicemail every time. Her battery may be dead.'

'Have you spoken to either of her employers?'

'Ja,' Dewald says – at last, something he's done right. 'Mr Robertson at the municipality said Imelda was there on Sunday night but not on Monday night. And I called the pharmacy, and they said she was there on Monday, and that she left work as usual at 4 p.m. So something must have happened to her after that.'

Cupido writes for some time, then stops. 'And you didn't report her missing for two days because …?'

'Oh, work,' he says. 'Extra shifts. The roadworks – I work at the quarry. I worked Sunday, Monday and Tuesday night. I didn't even realise Imelda was missing until this morning.'

'You and your wife don't phone each other?' the detective asks.

This time there's a light but very clear note of disbelief.

'We do, sometimes,' Dewald says, immediately defensive. 'We just didn't this time.' Even to him it doesn't sound credible.

Detective Cupido puts her pen down, and uses both hands to square the sheets of paper in front of her. Then she says, without looking at Dewald, 'Listen. It's always best to tell us everything. If we don't know everything, that gets in the way of finding the missing person, you understand?' She looks up at Dewald, holding eye contact for a few moments. Dewald notices there are flecks of yellow in her brown eyes.

'I've told you everything I know,' Dewald says. He feels his face heating up, and knows he's getting angry. He mustn't get angry – it won't help.

'So you're sure your wife isn't seeing someone else?' the detective asks. 'Maybe someone at work? This ...' she refers again to the statement she's putting together, paging back to find what she's looking for '... Mr Robertson?'

'God, no,' Dewald blurts. He hasn't met Robertson personally but he knows just from their brief phone exchange that he's the kind of person Imelda would hate: unhelpful, judgemental, snobby.

'Anyone at the pharmacy?'

'Look, Detective Cupido, I understand why you're asking me this, but I promise, Imelda isn't having an affair,' he says.

The detective purses her lips and nods but it's evident she's not convinced.

'What about her cellphone?' Dewald asks suddenly. 'Can't you trace it? Aren't there towers you can ping or something?' He's on shaky ground here, as he knows very little about cellphone technology, but he's sure he's read somewhere that even if a phone isn't charged, even if it's dead, it's still traceable as long as the battery is in it.

As if reading his thoughts, Cupido says, 'When the phone's battery is dead, that means it's not in contact with the network, so you wouldn't be able to locate it.' Then she smiles resignedly and adds, 'We don't have that kind of technology, anyway. We barely get the budget to buy stationery and replace broken chairs. No way is this little outpost going to qualify for cellphone trackers.'

Dewald tilts his head back and stares up at the ceiling. This feeling of helplessness is just unbearable.

The detective's voice, quiet now, breaks the short reverie. 'You do know that Mrs Uys, as a grownup, would be completely within her rights to just walk away? Adults are allowed to leave other adults if they want to. They don't have to give reasons or leave goodbye letters.'

'Imelda didn't leave me,' Dewald says. 'We're everything to each other. We're all each other has.'

Captain Cupido nods again, then leans back in her chair. She takes a deep breath and says, 'So, Mr Uys, if your wife isn't having an affair, and she didn't leave you for someone else, and she didn't just walk away, what do you think happened to her?'

It's a good question and Dewald has no answer to it.

Wednesday 24 February
1.13 p.m.

Back home, Dewald phones Imelda's cellphone again a couple of times. Voicemail.

Captain Cupido has said that she'll come out to their place later today, 'to have a look around', although what she could possibly find in their tiny house that could give her a clue as to Imelda's whereabouts, he doesn't know.

He suddenly realises that he's due back at the quarry at 4 p.m.

He calls his boss, who answers quickly, sounding surprised. As far as he can recall, Dewald has never phoned him.

'Sir, I can't come in later,' Dewald says, and this surprises his boss even more. Dewald has never, not once, missed a shift since he started working at the quarry about six years before. 'I've got a personal emergency I have to deal with.'

'No, that's okay,' the man says. 'I'll make a plan.'

Dewald is enormously grateful he hasn't asked what the 'personal emergency' is. It's becoming clear to him that the disappearance of his wife is something that most people might consider to be his fault in some way or another, either as if he's just been a crap husband and caused her to leave him for someone else, or for more sinister reasons; and the time lapse between her disappearance and his discovery of it is hard to explain and he can see how it looks suspicious, even if it's completely true.

When he disconnects the call, Dewald sits for a while and tries to think objectively about his and Imelda's relationship. With Vumba's big, soft head between his knees, his hands on her head and her wolf eyes fixed on his, he thinks to himself, Could there be something I'm missing? Could Imelda actually have run off with someone else?

He knows the answer, on a visceral level: absolutely not. But maybe other husbands have thought they've known the answer too, and have been wrong.

He goes into their bedroom and opens Imelda's bedside drawer. It's not as if it could hide any secrets – they both look in each other's bedside drawers all the time, for headache tablets or the phone charger or the nail clippers … But maybe he's missing something?

He examines all the familiar items: a nail file, a magnifying glass, a tube of lip salve, a small torch, a carry-around pack of tissues, her contraceptive pills (two of which, he thinks, by the way, she's now missed taking), three pairs of knitting needles of different sizes and colours, the last birthday card he got her – it's got a picture of a heart on the front, and the phrase 'If I had my life again …' and inside it says, '… I'd meet you sooner.' There's nothing that looks even the slightest bit odd or suspicious or out of place.

He moves across the room to the tallboy dresser, which they had bought at the town's secondhand furniture shop when they first moved into this rented house. Imelda has the top three drawers, he has the bottom three. He opens the top drawer, where she keeps her underwear. He rifles quickly through the panties and bras and socks – nothing. Next drawer down is scarves, and again, that's all that's in the drawer: scarves. Third drawer down is her jewellery in a cardboard box on one side, and her makeup in a matching cardboard box on the other. There's very little of either.

He feels a stabbing pain of sadness that they're living such a tiny life, that Imelda's stock of beautiful things, and things that she thinks make her look more beautiful, are so small. But, he reminds himself – as Imelda so often reminds him, when he becomes despondent or wants to spend money on something non-essential – it'll be worth it in the end.

He does a quick check of her clothing cupboards – nothing unusual in the hanging section, or among her neatly folded T-shirts, shorts and winter-wear on the shelves.

'Sorry, sweetie,' he whispers, feeling bad for doubting her.

Vumba, sitting at the door to the bedroom, watching him going through his wife's belongings, wags her tail at his voice. There's no judgement from her.

Wednesday 24 February
1.44 p.m.

The foreman takes a last bite of his apple, then tosses it away into the underbrush.

He's sitting with his back against the trunk of one of the bluegum trees in the copse off the old, chopped-up road, which lies between the trees and the new road up the hill where all the activity is happening. He's technically on private property, but all the fences have been taken down along this section of the road until the upgrade project is finished, so the usual rules don't really apply.

These eighteen soaring eucalyptus trees were once part of a much larger and longer windbreak planted by the original owner of Bloekom Farm almost seventy years ago. Hardy and fast-growing, bluegums – although not native to this area or even this country, and deeply greedy when it comes to their water needs – were once much loved by farmers as windbreaks. The tall evergreens with their strong, straight trunks whose pale bark peels away in papery strips, exposing rich yellowish-brown patches that harden and fade over time, also made for impressive colonnaded driveways, lining either side of an entry road to a farmyard.

Happy in very hot climates, the leaves of bluegums are dark green and glossy above, paler below. They face downwards, partly to prevent direct exposure to sunlight and thus loss of water.

Bees love these trees. The nectar gathered from their blooms makes a delicious, mild honey. But other flying insects aren't as partial: the pungent natural oils of the bluegum act as a mosquito repellent, hence the lack of those annoying biting bugs in this copse.

The foreman doesn't know any of this as he sits in the welcome shade of the one of the tall trees, mercifully some distance away from the commotion of the roadworks. He's just too happy to be out of the heat and dust for a while. He also doesn't know that when the current owner bought the farm about twenty years ago, he cut down most of the kilometre-long windbreak, using some of the timber harvested from the mature bluegums to build several sturdy structures on the farm (all still standing) and selling the rest to a timber mill for a very useful sum.

He left this copse of eighteen trees at the entrance to the farm as a kind of visual signboard, and for many years it was the only thing that identified the farm; he'd only had the actual sign for Bloekom Farm made and wired to the gate in 2010, six years ago. But now the gate, and the fence for several kilometres on either side, has been dismantled and removed by the roadbuilding crew, who will be installing concrete gulleys along what was the fence line to efficiently deal with stormwater for if and when proper rains ever return to this part of the country. In the second year of this horrendous drought, that seems right now to be an improbability at best.

The deal the authorities have struck with the farmer is that once the building of the dual carriageway is complete, and the stormwater gulleys installed, his fence and gate will be replaced, as good as new. In the meantime, the copse of eucalyptus is back to doing its job of informing would-be visitors of the precise location of the entrance to Bloekom Farm off the national road.

The foreman hears a shout and looks up. It's the guy who's doing the shuttering along the sides of the new road, prepping it for pouring the concrete. He makes a 'come here' gesture.

The foreman clicks his tongue. This guy can't do anything without him holding his hand. But he stands up, hearing the snapping sounds in his knees over the cicada chorus that's blasting out of the eucalyptus stand, and makes his way back to the new road, walking slowly up the steepish hill to the old road, then carefully navigating through the chopped-up piles of tarmac.

Jissis, it's hot.

He's lived in these parts for most of his adult life, and he's used to the crazy-hot summers, but this one takes the cake. He nudges a piece of the old tarmac with his work boot, and sure enough, it sticks – the sun is hot enough to literally melt tarmac.

The drought has made things worse – they've had to carefully monitor drinking water, and they haven't been allowed to use the municipal supply for the road construction, because the reservoir levels have dropped so low, and the river too, so they've had to bring in their own, recycled, water in bowsers.

Reaching the new road, the foreman meets up with the shuttering guy. 'Ja? What's the problem?' he asks.

Down in the copse of bluegum trees, not ten metres from where the foreman was sitting moments before, the little blue car hangs upside down in its hammock of branches.

The temperature inside is once again in the forties.

The body trapped in the driver's seat hasn't moved in more than a day.

Wednesday 24 February
2.49 p.m.

Dewald hears car tyres crunching on the gravel drive outside the house, and he rushes to the front door, Vumba on his heels. But it's not Imelda's little VW; it's a police patrol van, and he can see Detective Cupido in the driver's seat. She's early.

She notices Dewald glance at his watch, and winds down the driver's window to call out, 'Things were slow at the station.'

Dewald nods. Good, he thinks. Let's get this search going.

Cupido hasn't told him there's going to be a search, but he assumes that now that the missing-person paperwork has been completed, the actual search will begin. And, he thinks, of course Detective Cupido would want to start with their home – it's where he last saw his wife, after all.

'That dog friendly?' Cupido asks, nodding her head towards Vumba, who's circling the vehicle on loping legs, sniffing the wheels.

'Ja,' Dewald replies. 'Not a mean bone in her body. She only looks like she might eat you.'

Cupido doesn't seem completely convinced, and Dewald understands that: before Vumba, he wasn't that keen on dogs either.

Vumba had been the pet of a colleague at the quarry, raised with the kids and much loved by her family. The guy's youngest, a toddler, had drowned in a bucket of recycled water placed in the bathroom for use to flush the toilet. It was an unthinkable tragedy, ghastly collateral damage of the water shortage, and it had shattered the family. The guy's wife had left him and taken their other two kids, and he'd eventually sold their family home and moved into a flat. Dewald had volunteered to look after Vumba for a while, until the guy got himself sorted out, and a while has turned into almost a year now, and the guy, who is still in the flat and doesn't look like he's going to get himself sorted out any time soon, has stopped asking how the dog is doing.

As it happens, she's doing just fine. She's an incredibly chilled animal, and although her size, wolf-like demeanour and jet-black pelt give her the appearance of an attack-dog, nothing could be further from the truth. Her endearingly mismatched ears, one ever erect, the other permanently flopped over, are a clue to her real personality, which is both fiercely intelligent and protective, and ridiculously laid back.

She'd taken to Dewald immediately, and apparently accepted him as her new owner without a backward glance at her previous life. She's happy with him and Imelda as long as they feed her and pay some attention to her occasionally. While they're both at work, she's content to snooze away the hours inside, and she seems equally happy on her walks with Dewald, which he takes her on whenever he can find time. She seems to just have the most amazing trust that everything will always turn out fine in the end, and Dewald often finds himself looking at her with admiration but also something approaching envy. He certainly could do with a big dose of that trust right now.

Dewald watches Captain Cupido stride over to him, studiously ignoring Vumba, who's sniffing searchingly around her ankles. Now that she isn't sitting behind a counter, Dewald notices that the police officer is short and squat, with squarish hands – they make her look strong and capable. He likes the confidence in her walk, too – he has a feeling that if anyone can find his wife, it's this woman.

She shakes his hand firmly and gestures with her chin at the open front door. 'Should we go inside?'

They take a seat in the breakfast nook, which puts them in uncomfortably close quarters. It's fine when Imelda is sitting practically in his lap but Dewald isn't sure how to deal with having the detective's frank gaze so close to his.

Vumba pushes her long black nose between them, for which Dewald is grateful. He offers her a hand to lick, to keep her there.

'Okay, so,' Detective Cupido begins. 'Your wife disappeared on Monday evening. You didn't report her missing until today.'

'Ja, and I told you why,' Dewald says, wishing he didn't sound so defensive.

'Ja,' Cupido says, pushing herself back in the chair, then turning and stretching her legs out in front of her before crossing them at the ankle. The kitchen is so small that, short as she is, her boots are now more or less in the middle of the room. 'But how do I know you didn't kill her, Mr Uys?'

The suggestion floors Dewald. '*What?*' he says.

'Well, it looks suspicious,' Captain Cupido replies, casually linking her hands behind her head. 'You say you and your wife are like this' – she briefly holds up her right hand, entwining her pointer and middle finger – 'but somehow you don't even notice she's gone for two days and two nights?'

'But I explained that,' Dewald says, feeling anger working its way up from somewhere in his stomach area towards his jaw. 'I was working. We often don't see each other for—'

'Ja, but still,' Cupido cuts him off. 'You see how it looks, hey?'

Dewald stares at the detective, defensive, furious and appalled, as she continues.

'I've spoken to Mr Roberts at the municipality – a real charmer, that one.' She rolls her eyes. 'He told me the same thing he told you, that Mrs Uys had signed in and signed out at what seemed like normal times. What he couldn't tell me was that he'd seen her himself with his very own eyes.'

Dewald is working at tamping down the anger. He doesn't

want to give this detective any reason to believe he may have had anything at all to do with Mel's disappearance. In fact, he needs to find a way to convince her not to waste her time on investigating him, but to turn her attention to other possibilities. But he's struggling to find words, as usual. Then he thinks of something: 'But she was at work on Monday at the pharmacy,' he points out.

'True, true,' Cupido muses. 'And she left at the usual time, according to Yolande February, who I also spoke to.'

'Ja, and I don't think she got home that night because of the pillows and the toothbrushes,' Dewald says, 'and the laundry. So I think something happened to her after she left the pharmacy.'

Ignoring this observation, Cupido says, 'I've spoken to your boss, too,' her tone level and studiedly uninterested. Unlinking her hands from behind her head and straightening up in the chair, she removes a notebook from her top pocket, flips it to a certain page, and refers to it. 'He's confirmed that you worked from Sunday night 9 p.m. to Monday morning 9 a.m., then on Monday from 4 p.m. to 10 p.m., and again from midnight to 6 a.m. on Tuesday morning. Then you helped him fill out the paperwork for orders until 8 a.m even though it isn't part of your job.'

Dewald is nodding – yes, yes, yes.

'So you came home on Tuesday morning but you didn't notice that your wife wasn't here?'

'No, because *that's normal*,' Dewald says, a little wildly. This is driving him crazy. 'By the time I got home it was well past 8 a.m. Her shift at the pharmacy is 8.30 a.m. to 4 p.m. She would've already left – if she'd been here, I mean.'

Cupido continues, her face as usual giving nothing away. 'On Tuesday you worked 4 p.m. to 10 p.m. again, and midnight to 6 a.m. again.' She looks up and Dewald nods again. 'What did you do in those two free hours?' she asks.

'What? I rested in the break room,' says Dewald, hearing the pitch of his voice rising with exasperation and worrying that the detective is going to read something else into it. 'There are a couple of stretchers in there. The boss saw me there, he'll tell you.'

'Okay, okay,' Cupido says, holding up a conciliatory hand to show she believes him. 'But you didn't leave work at six on Wednesday morning, hey?'

'There was an injury in the quarry. Someone slipped and broke his ankle. I had to fill in the paperwork for that.'

'So you got home on Wednesday morning around 8 a.m. and only then noticed for the first time that your wife was missing?'

'Ja,' Dewald says. 'At first I thought I'd just missed her but, I don't know, the house felt ... weird. Weirdly empty. There was no smell of toast or coffee or anything. And the pillows and the toothbrushes ...' He trails off.

'Which you didn't notice on the Tuesday?' Cupido asks.

Dewald shakes his head. 'You're making it sound like I stayed late on purpose after my shifts, that I got home late on purpose,' he says, flustered. 'The quarry is so busy, everyone's doing a bit extra. And I was the safety officer on duty on Tuesday night – I had no choice about filling in those forms – it's a legal thing.' He stops and takes a short, sharp breath, then shakes his head. 'Seriously, you're wasting your time with me. I didn't do anything to my wife. Can't you give me a polygraph or something?'

Cupido scoffs. 'Our polygraph machine is in the same parallel universe as our cellphone tracker,' she says.

The two people stare at each other across the very short gap separating them, Cupido unwavering, Dewald feeling the beginnings of a tic in the bottom lid of his left eye. Vumba sighs and plonks her big head on his thigh. Distractedly, Dewald fondles her uneven ears.

'What if she was kidnapped?' he asks suddenly.

Detective Cupido gives a curt nod that Dewald isn't sure how to interpret. 'What for? Do you have lots of money?' He can see she's actively avoiding looking pointedly around the tiny, sparsely furnished kitchen.

Dewald gives a short laugh and says, 'I know how stupid it sounds but what else could have happened to her? People don't just disappear.'

'They do if someone wants to disappear them,' Cupido says.

He exhales with a despairing whooshing sound, letting his cheeks puff out, and rubs a hand over his face. His eyes feel prickly with exhaustion. 'I didn't kill my wife,' he says, slowly. 'I don't know how to make you believe me but I didn't kill her.'

'So why would someone have kidnapped her?'

'I don't know.' He shakes his head. He knows the idea is preposterous. 'Maybe ...' Dewald has given this some thought but it's very hard for him to put into words – he doesn't want to give the idea any kind of concrete form. 'What if someone raped her, then killed her so she wouldn't tell?'

'It's always a possibility,' the detective says, her tone even. Then she returns her little notebook to her top pocket and shifts in her chair, indicating a new thought. 'Has anyone shown an unusual interest in your wife recently? Any odd phone calls? Anything that could be interpreted as stalker behaviour?'

Dewald is shaking his head at her first question – although now that he thinks about it, he and Imelda actually spend so little waking time together that he's not sure he would know if someone was stalking her or not. (And does it then follow that he wouldn't know if she were seeing someone else?)

'No,' he replies, answering his own thoughts as much as the detective's questions. 'Imelda is quiet, shy. She wouldn't attract that kind of attention.'

Cupido nods. 'Right,' she says, clapping both hands down on her thighs. Vumba looks at her, interested. 'Mind if I poke around a bit?'

'Sure,' Dewald says. He's only too keen to show the detective that he's genuinely got nothing to hide.

She gets up, Vumba on her heels, and moves into the bedroom. Dewald can hear drawers opening and closing.

'She's pretty,' he hears the detective say, and Dewald realises that she must be looking at their wedding photo, which stands on top of the tallboy. It was taken outside the municipality on the big day by the student who'd served as a witness, using Dewald's cellphone. Imelda had printed it out quite recently, surreptitiously, at the municipality, and carefully positioned it in a secondhand picture frame she'd found in a junk shop.

He hears her go into the bathroom, and the cabinet doors opening and shutting – there's nothing in there but some headache pills, toothpaste, shaving gear and Imelda's moisturiser.

She comes back into the living room, Vumba her shadow, and says, 'I'm just going to have a look around outside.'

Dewald stands up and goes with her to the back door, and watches her as she takes a turn around the tiny back yard, dogged by the dog. She pokes in the ashes of the braai, and stoops to examine one or two areas more closely. There are, Dewald realises, more than two days' worth of Vumba's turds dotted around. He hasn't been out here to pick them up since he and Imelda braaied on Sunday.

Cupido stands up and rubs her chin, then seems to come to some sort of conclusion. 'You say you think she disappeared after work on Monday?'

'As far as I can tell,' Dewald says.

'And, as far as you can tell, there was nothing out of place here in the house – no signs of a struggle, nothing like that …?'

'No.'

'So it's fair to assume that she disappeared some time between leaving her job at the pharmacy just after 4 p.m. on Monday afternoon, and when she should have got home around …?'

Dewald stares at the detective, then realises she's waiting for him to fill in the blank. 'Five-ish, I suppose,' he says. 'She's usually already home when I get home from the quarry but I've been doing extra …'

The detective waves her hand at him. 'Extra shifts, I know, I know,' she says. Then she walks back towards him where he's standing at the back door and says, 'Let's take a drive.'

Wednesday 24 February
4.03 p.m.

Dewald Uys and Detective Cupido stand on the town square, looking over the serried rows of neatly parked vehicles, near the pharmacy where Imelda works.

A few years ago the municipality upgraded the square. It was a big project that involved tarring over sections of it for formal parking, planting some trees and installing a drinking fountain. The tarred parking and trees were much needed. Before that, the square had turned into a mudbath in winter, the reddish clayey soil churned up by the wheels of dozens of vehicles daily. In summer it was a scorching dustbowl. The drinking fountain was less successful, doing double duty as a makeshift laundry, cooling-off spot and occasional lavatory for the town indigents. Now, in the drought, it has been turned off.

'Keep your eyes open for anything that looks, you know, out of place,' Cupido says, using her head to gesture around the square. 'I don't think that if your wife was kidnapped or murdered, the kidnapper or murderer would be here again today, but you never know.' She glances at Dewald and catches his horrified expression; she must try to remember that most of the public aren't used to the kinds of things she's exposed to all the time in her work. 'Sorry,' she mutters. She looks at her watch. 'Then let's leave here when she did,' she says. 'We'll give it a couple of minutes.'

Dewald, still shaken, nods slightly and leans up against the police van, then glances around in what he hopes is a casual manner. People of all different shapes, colours, genders, hairstyles, dress and attitude are coming and going, getting into and out of a huge range of vehicles – farm bakkies like his, little runarounds like Imelda's, big foreign fancy cars, delivery vans, motorbikes …

'Needle in a haystack,' he mutters, and Cupido nods.

'I don't expect we'll see anything helpful here,' she acknowledges. 'Come, let's go.'

They get back into the police van and begin the drive back to the Uyses' house along the national road.

Within a kilometre of the town's outer limits there's a stop-go, and they join the queue of cars waiting for the oncoming traffic to clear the single lane in use.

'Been a while, these roadworks,' Imelda says as they wait.

'Mm-hm.'

'Created plenty jobs – but you know that.'

'Mm-hm.'

'You worked in the quarry before the roadworks started?'

Dewald glances at her – is this a loaded question? But she's staring through the windscreen so he can't read her expression. 'No,' he replies.

'So where did you work?'

'In the city.'

'Doing what?'

'I worked for a building contractor,' he says, then adds, 'Is this an interrogation? Why does any of this matter?'

Cupido shrugs. 'Just passing the time,' she says pleasantly.

The woman operating the stop-go system flips the sign from red to green, and waves on the line of cars. The detective puts the van in gear, and they move off slowly.

Dewald stares out the window while Cupido, driving, is careful to keep her distance from a huge lorry carrying sand which sprays out liquid-like in the vehicle's wake. She glances at her passenger then swivels her head, indicating everything around them. 'Just look at this activity – people for Africa, roadworks vehicles, lots of traffic sharing this temporary road … It's hard to believe that one day, fairly soon, cars are just going to whizz by on what will be a giant highway.'

'They must be so proud,' Dewald says sarcastically. Jissis, this is irritating, he thinks. He wishes Cupido would stop prattling.

'What I'm also trying to say is that if your wife had some kind of accident along this stretch of road, which is something we've got to regard as a possibility, someone would've seen it. It probably would've involved another car or a truck or a lorry – or maybe even a person. But what I'm saying is that it would've been reported – we would know about it.'

'Oh,' Dewald responds. 'Ja. But I did do this drive both ways twice this morning, once when I came in to buy the charger and then when I came in to report …' Dewald looks uncomfortable, then says simply, 'it,' then continues, 'and we've just done it again coming in. I didn't see any signs of an accident along the road, so I'd kind of written that off as a possibility.'

'Right,' the detective says. 'I'm just saying.'

Dewald, his limbs suddenly leaden with tiredness, slumps in the passenger seat. He just wants to get home and he wants Imelda to be there when he does, and he wants his life to go back to the way it was before this terrible day began.

'You know why I don't think you killed your wife?' Cupido asks.

Dewald sighs. 'Why?'

'Because I checked for both of you on Facebook this morning but you're not there, and you're not on Instagram or any other social media. And I posted a note about Imelda's disappearance on the town's Facebook page, and I didn't get a single response – nobody seems to know who either of you are, and nobody's got any theories about where your wife has gone. And, believe me, there's usually no shortage of theories about anything and everything on the town's Facebook page.'

Dewald doesn't say anything. He and Imelda aren't on any social-media sites because they don't feel the need to share anything about their lives with the world at large. They are simply perfectly happy in each other's company.

'So you two live in your own world. You're everything to each other,' the detective continues. 'Which is fine, you know. But if you did kill her, it doesn't seem anyone else would really have noticed, and you would've probably got away with it by just keeping your mouth shut. You could probably have made up a plausible reason for her absence from both her jobs, and been believed – her employers seem to know almost nothing about her. So if you did kill her, what would the point have been in coming to the police?' She pauses and looks at Dewald and adds, 'No offence intended.'

'None taken,' he replies automatically.

Wednesday 24 February
4.51 p.m.

'We'll be in touch,' says Captain Cupido, and she waves as she drives away from the little house. She's left Dewald her personal cellphone number, with instructions to call if 'anything turns up' – 'anything' being his beloved wife – but he can tell that she doesn't really expect to hear from him.

It's just been a wasted few hours, Dewald thinks, standing on the front step, Vumba beside him, watching the van disappear down the road and round the corner. So now the police know that his wife is gone, apparently without trace – and they seem to think that she's so inconsequential to anybody other than him that nobody but he misses her – but nobody seems to be doing anything about it.

He suddenly realises he's hungry – he hasn't eaten since last night. He goes inside and puts a couple of slices of bread in the toaster, then pulls the margarine out the fridge and the peanut butter out of cupboard.

He wolfs down the two slices of peanut-butter toast, then makes two more and eats those too, standing at the kitchen nook.

He refills Vumba's food bowl, cueing signs of real excitement from the world's most relaxed dog, then phones Imelda's cellphone again a few times. Voicemail every time.

Just this last weekend, he would have sworn with one hundred percent certainty that there was no-one significant in Imelda's life but he himself. He thought he knew about his wife everything it was possible for one person to know about another. They really are everything to each other: they are each other's proverbial stars and moon.

But how much is it actually possible for one person to know

about another? Dewald thinks, turning the cellphone idly over and over in his hands. Mel doesn't know, for example, that he really hated all the driving between the quarry and the chemist and the municipality and home, back before she had her licence. He had always told her that he didn't mind, but he did. And it had started to make him resent her. That's why he'd suggested that they buy another car and Mel get her licence.

He'd told her that another car would free him up to take on more shifts, so they could put away more money, but that wasn't the real reason. The real reason was that he just didn't want to do all that driving any more. He couldn't stand it. The roadworks made every trip a nightmare, and it got to the point where when Mel was chatting to him on those endless trips, he would feel so irritated with her that it took all his self-control not to tell her to shut up.

Shame makes his shoulders slump as he recalls his hidden irritability, how his sweet wife would prattle on, oblivious of his feelings of resentment, thinking that his silence or, at best, monosyllabic answers were just part of his naturally quiet personality.

Dewald's guilt is accompanied by another unpleasant emotion, one he's never experienced before when it comes to his wife: suspicion. If he was able to hide those strong feelings from Mel, what could she be hiding from him?

He groans out loud and sinks into one of the little kitchen chairs. 'No, man,' he says to himself, putting the cellphone firmly on the breakfast-nook counter. 'Don't be stupid.' His wife isn't cheating on him. She hasn't left him. She hasn't run away. Of that, he's … ninety-nine percent sure.

'But then where the fuck is she?' he asks the room, not bothering to sanitise the swear word. It's not like Mel would know – she isn't here to hear him.

And then he's back to guilt again, because he knows Mel wouldn't like to know that he's swearing.

'Please be alive,' he whispers to himself, and is immediately mortified by the selfishness of the thought. 'Or please be dead if it means it will spare you terrible pain,' he adds.

His tone is so full of aching that even Vumba, absorbed in her food, stops munching for a moment and looks at him.

He stands up and walks across the tiny room to the small wall-mounted TV. They only get the local stations, which are all rubbish, but right now he needs distraction to drown out these excruciating thoughts.

He switches it on. It's the news. There's a story about some huge political graft; Dewald and Imelda aren't political people and they don't follow their country's politics, but they're aware that they live in a time of larceny on such a grand scale that it seems just plain stupid to pay taxes (but of course they both do). There's a story of a mine collapse; two dead. There's a story of a 5-year-old who's won an international singing contest. There's a story of two local girls who went missing six years ago and have just been found in the river.

Dewald switches off the TV. He goes into the little bedroom and lies down on the bed. He's so tired but he doesn't think he can sleep.

But he's out in a few minutes.

Tamara Cupido takes longer to nod off. The detective enjoys a good puzzle – it's practically a prerequisite of the job – but she doesn't like those that seem to have no solution. And the vanishing of Imelda Uys apparently fits into that category.

There are so many terrible things that may have happened to her, had she fallen foul of a criminal: abduction, assault, rape, torture, murder, each possibility rife with subcategories of horror, their depth and extent dependent only on the imagination and depravity of the perpetrator. But sophistication isn't a characteristic of most of the lawbreakers around these parts. Those who commit heinous crimes to feed a drug habit are by far in the majority, and they're always careless and disorganised. If she'd fallen victim to one of these, Imelda's body would almost certainly already have been found.

In the years Cupido has been working this beat, there hasn't been a serial murderer. The only serial sexual predator she knows of was Allan Knotwood, who'd targeted that most vulnerable group – impoverished children, poor little girls.

Lying awake, staring the ceiling of her bedroom in the tiny house she still shares with her elderly parents, Captain Cupido more or less dismisses abduction as a possible cause of Imelda Uys's disappearance – as she's discussed with the husband, there's no credible motive for such an eventuality.

Kicking the duvet away from her overheating body, then turning onto her side and closing her eyes, the detective lets her thoughts drift to the whims of the universe, the reality of a lived existence surrounded by objects and forces, often operating entirely without human agency but which sometimes seem out to get us. She recalls the story of the mother and daughter, driving in their little car into the city from the suburbs, on their way to work and school, the same way they'd done so many times before. It was the windy season, with gale-force gusts of over a hundred kilometres per hour regularly disrupting traffic. As the mother and daughter drew abreast of, then began passing, a huge flatbed truck stacked high with long wooden logs, just such a wind blew up. In an accident so unexpected and horrific that it was unthinkable, the truck blew over, crushing the little car and its occupants.

And it doesn't even have to be a force as strong as a mighty wind. Good old gravity has played its fair share of fatal tricks on humans. The pastor's young helper at the church she'd gone to as a child had been killed when a small upright piano they were moving from the donor's house to the church hall tumbled out of the back of the truck and onto his head.

In a jangling decrescendo of discordant musical notes, Cupido surrenders to sleep.

Wednesday 24 February
9.12 p.m.

All is quiet in the copse of trees where the little blue car is still lodged, upside down, in its hammock of branches.

The sun-loving cicadas are sitting quiet, their synchronised songs – an impressive group effort to attract mates – temporarily silenced.

The hammering heat has also ever so slightly softened, replaced by a still, hot dryness.

The body inside the car hasn't moved for a very, very long time, but now its eyelids flicker. The eyes don't open – they can't; they're too swollen. The cracked lips part slightly and a sound emerges on the slight exhalation, but if it's a word it's too soft and too badly formed in the punished mouth with its puffy, injured tongue to hear what it is.

The new road isn't far from the copse of trees – just forty metres or so. It's only been open since Monday evening, and the occasional car passes by on it travelling smoothly on its new surface. Sometimes there's a larger vehicle, a bus or a lorry, carrying people and goods between the city and the northern towns and up to the border. This new road, currently serving as a temporary two-way thoroughfare, will eventually become the southbound – the city-bound – side of the dual carriageway.

The old road, which lies between the new road and the copse of bluegums, has been closed since Monday evening. Yesterday, a huge digger-loader was used to excavate the old tarmac, which now lies in piles where a usable road used to be. No more work will be done on this old road until next week, when the tarmac will be removed and the lengthy process of turning the old road into the new northbound – border-bound – dual carriageway will begin.

Thursday 25 February
2.16 a.m.

Dewald wakes up from a dream of being trapped. It's a recurring one, one he's had since childhood, and even he can work out that it's not unrelated to his father's favourite punishment: locking him, sometimes for hours, in the dark, spider-infested single garage crowded from floor to ceiling with old furniture and other junk, at the far end of their plot. It was too far away from the house – or any other inhabited structure in the remote rural area he grew up in – for anyone to hear his desperate, terrified screams.

He's lying in dampness, and realises he's seriously overheating – he must have fallen asleep with the duvet over him, and now his body is drenched in sweat. A cloud of buzzing mosquitoes hangs above him, and he's suddenly aware of pinpricks on his arms and legs – they're having a feast.

He throws the duvet off and leaps from the bed, waving his arms. Vumba comes loping through, slightly interested.

He goes into the kitchen, opens the back door, and sits down on the step looking into the little back yard, nervously nibbling the insides of his cheeks. The night is hot. There's no relief of even a little breeze, but it's slightly cooler out here than inside.

He watches Vumba quarter the back yard in that way dogs do when they're looking for a place to have a crap, and reminds himself to pick up all the dog turds tomorrow morning.

He wishes he still smoked – he's dying for a cigarette right now. He gave up when he met Imelda. Imelda's mother had been a heavy smoker, and the two of them had worked hard to help each other eliminate all reminders of their similarly grim childhoods.

'Flip, Mel, where are you?' he says into the blackness of the back garden. It's a moonless night and densely dark.

Swearing – that's another thing he's given up for Imelda.

No, that's not right, he tells himself: 'gave up', 'giving up' – that sounds like a defeat, or a favour. It's neither. It's leaving behind behaviours that Imelda associates negatively with her mother's neglect and abuse. And what's the harm in leaving behind smoking and swearing? None.

Imelda has given up things for him. Her virginity, for one. He thinks back to their wedding night, and the surprising tenderness of it, and the memory gives him an actual pain in the pit of his stomach.

'*Where are you, Mel?*' he shouts suddenly, tipping his head back so the question flies into the dark night.

A nearby dog barks once, twice. Vumba momentarily pricks up her uneven ears – the floppy one makes it erect for a couple of seconds before drooping over again – but shows no other reaction.

And there's no other response.

Back in the house, Dewald puts on the kettle. He's not going to get back to sleep.

He switches on the TV, and the same news cycle is repeating itself: political graft, mine collapse, 5-year-old singing star, missing girls found after six years …

Wait.

Dewald leans forward and turns up the volume.

'It is thought that the car in which the two girls were travelling, on their way to a party on a farm in July 2010, flipped off a bridge into a flooded river. The car remained hidden beneath the water until two days ago, when the ongoing drought caused the water level to drop and brought the wheels of the vehicle into view.' The newsreader – a different one from this morning – isn't making eye contact with the camera, but has her head down, reading from a sheet of paper. 'The 2006 Ford Fiesta, which was found on Tuesday afternoon, was in gear, with the headlights in the on position.'

Now the TV is flashing images of a bag of some sort, some clothing and a driver's licence that shows a smiling young woman. The newsreader's voice continues, 'The car contained the remains of Rosanne Bronson and Jess Hallett, both 17-year-olds from a nearby town.'

Back to the newsreader, now reading from the teleprompter: 'The disappearance of the girls in July 2010 was investigated at the time. Ryan Chapel, who lived at the farm and was a classmate of the girls, was initially thought to have been involved in the disappearance, but was later cleared.

'It is thought that the heavy winter rains of 2010 washed the car about a kilometre downriver of the bridge, where it sank from sight in a deeper section. Coincidentally, the Ford Fiesta was discovered in the river directly opposite the entrance to the Chapel farm.

'Ryan Chapel and his father, Charlie "Vlieg" Chapel, are now both serving unrelated sentences, for drug dealing and car theft, respectively.'

The newsreader flashes a toothpaste smile at the camera, and says, 'And now for the weather …'

Dewald turns down the volume and sits quite still for some time, staring at the TV, thinking carefully about what the newsreader has said. Two girls, driving from point A and expected at point B, vanished without trace. Although their disappearance was investigated at the time, they couldn't be found, and there seemed to be no explanation for their vanishing. They've now been found, and all indications are that their car simply flipped off the road and into the river, then floated some distance downstream before rapidly sinking from sight – totally out of view of anyone who happened to be passing or even someone actively looking for the car.

'Flip,' Dewald says.

Thursday 25 February
3.11 a.m.

'Ja?' The voice is muffled with sleep.

'It's Dewald Uys. I'm sorry to call you so late but I have to—'

'Jissis, man, it's three in the morning. Call me when it's real day.'

'*Wait! Please, I have to speak to you!*' Dewald shouts into the cellphone.

'Seriously, man? It can't wait until the sun gets up?'

Dewald, sitting on the edge of the double bed in the little bedroom, is so desperate for Captain Cupido to hear his theory that he grasps the sheet in his left hand, squeezing and crumpling it spasmodically. 'I'm begging you, please listen.'

Vumba, registering this new and concerning tone in her master's voice, wags her tail once, uncertainly, then sits, her eyes fixed on Dewald's face.

'Jissis,' Cupido says again. 'This better be good.'

'Look, I've just seen that story on TV, about the girls whose car went into the river? Bronson was the name of one, I can't remember the other. You know it?'

'Ja, it was one of my cases,' Cupido says. 'Dead ends wherever we looked. Then the car comes out of the water like the Lady of the Lake.'

The reference means nothing to Dewald but he doesn't care: the detective knows the case.

'Okay, so, no foul play, hey? The car hit something and flipped over the bridge?'

'Ja,' Cupido says. She hasn't thought about that case in a few years although, of course, with the car being found, it's all come back to her. Ryan Chapel and his father, Charlie, selling drugs and stealing cars. Rosanne Bronson and Jess Hallett, gone without trace. 'Then the river carried it downstream. Most

195

people underestimate the power of water. If it's moving fast enough, fifteen centimetres can knock a person over, and only about double that would be enough to carry away most cars.' If Dewald is impressed by the detective's spontaneous sharing of the physics of floodwaters, he doesn't let on. Cupido continues, 'The forensics guys found nothing wrong with the engine that wouldn't have been caused by six years underwater. And the car was still in third gear when they found it.'

'And the headlights were on,' adds Dewald.

'Ja, well, in the on position.'

'So what if the same thing happened to Imelda?'

There's a short pause, then the detective barks out a laugh. 'There's no river on the stretch of road your wife travelled every day, Mr Uys.'

'No, but she was tired, you know. She has two jobs. She never gets enough sleep. What if she just fell asleep at the wheel and the car ran off the road?'

Cupido sighs. 'We drove that route yesterday, Mr Uys. You saw how much activity is going on there. If a car had run off the road, someone would've seen it.'

'But what if the car went into a ditch or something? What if it got hidden, like the Bronson girl's car?' Dewald so desperately wants the detective to buy into his story. It's the only theory that makes sense to him. It's the only one he's prepared to entertain as a possibility of what's happened to his wife. It's the only one left.

'Look, if it makes you feel any better, we can drive the route again tomorrow. We'll do it slowly and look carefully, and we'll ask around, okay?'

'Thank you!' says Dewald, his eyes filling with tears of gratitude, relief, desperation. 'I'll be at the police station at seven.'

'I don't get to work until eight,' the detective is saying, but Dewald has already disconnected the call.

Thursday 25 February
6.49 a.m.

When Detective Cupido pulls into the police station parking lot, she immediately sees Dewald Uys's battered white bakkie, with him standing next to it. She pulls into the parking space next to him and climbs out of the police van.

'I thought you'd be here early,' she says.

'Thanks for coming in early,' Dewald says at the same time.

'Let me just tell the duty officer I'm here, then we'll go,' says the detective.

Five minutes later, they're in Captain Cupido's van, heading out of town, back towards the Uyses' place, for the second time. For Dewald, it's the fourth time he's done this trip.

'So, according to your theory, what are we looking for?' Cupido asks.

'I don't know,' Dewald admits. 'A place where, if Mel fell asleep at the wheel and the car drove off the road, it may be hidden – like in a ditch or something.'

'She was on the road during peak-hour traffic, as far as we know,' says the detective. 'You don't think someone would've seen a car drive off the road?'

'What if she was going quite fast, and it happened in one of the dips?' Dewald says. He's been up most of the night, thinking through these various scenarios. 'The car is on the road one second, gone the next, and by the time the next vehicle comes past, there's no sign of it.'

'Ja, maybe,' says Cupido, in a tone that makes it clear she doesn't buy it.

'Drive slowly,' says Dewald, who's scanning both sides of the road as they travel along it.

'Like I have a choice,' Cupido comments, poking her chin at

the truck in front of them, which is trundling along sluggishly.

But even when the lorry turns off onto a cleared section next to the new road where there's already plenty of activity despite the early hour, Cupido keeps her speed under forty, giving Dewald plenty of time to carefully examine either side of the road.

Their slow trip from town to the turnoff into the little community where the Uyses live takes about forty-five minutes.

Detective Cupido pulls into the gravel driveway and kills the motor. The two sit in silence for a while, listening to the *tick-tick* of the engine cooling down.

'The problem is that where there are rises in the road, they've dug down to level out the new road, and where there are dips, they've filled them in, so now there are built-up embankments,' Dewald finally says, disappointment heavy in his voice. 'So, in almost all the places she might have gone to sleep and lost control of the car, it's actually physically impossible for the car to have left the road.'

'Ja,' Cupido says. She gazes out the window at the couple's little house, then glances at her passenger. 'Look, I know you don't want to think this way, but are you sure she didn't just leave? It happens, you know. Maybe she just got tired of it all – not having enough money, working all the time—'

'*No!*' Dewald exclaims, then adds more softly, 'No.' He rubs his eyes, then bumps the back of his head once, twice, three times against the passenger headrest. 'We have a five-year plan,' he says. 'We worked it out together two years ago. That's why things are so tight at the moment, and why we're both taking all the extra work we can get. We're saving money for a deposit on a house. It's not like we didn't know what we were getting into – we both knew it was going to be tough, but it'll be worth it in the end. Neither of us has ever owned anything. We want to own our own house. We want our own home.'

It's the longest stretch of words strung together that the detective has yet heard from Dewald, and he sounds so convinced that she wants to believe it too. But she's been a police officer for almost eight years now, and she's seen and heard things that defy belief. She doesn't disillusion him, however. She just nods and restarts the van.

They're forced to drive slowly on the return trip, as they become part of peak-hour morning traffic, with the roadworks restricting the flow and at the same time producing the occasional idiot overtaking on a blind rise or impatiently and dangerously tailgating. Dewald continues scanning either side of the road, looking for ditches into which a small blue car may have disappeared.

By the time they get back to the police station in town, he's feeling tearful and furious with defeat.

When he gets into his bakkie, Captain Cupido comes and stands at his window. 'Mr Uys, I'm prepared to believe you when you say that Mrs Uys wasn't having an affair and didn't just leave you,' she says. 'I also don't think you killed her. So that leaves only one possibility, and it's one we're going to have to aggressively pursue from this point on,' she says.

'You think she's been killed by someone else,' Dewald says, dully.

'Yes. We've got our list of usual suspects, of course, and we'll question them, but there's also the chance that it was an isolated incident, that Mrs Uys was just in the wrong place at the wrong time.'

'What does that mean?' Dewald asks.

The detective sighs and says, 'We've got a *lot* of open cases.'

In the station house, Captain Cupido makes herself a cup of nasty coffee and thinks about those open cases. The serious ones include several murders, some of them particularly gruesome.

The first of these, dating back some years, had shocked Cupido: an elderly man had been bludgeoned to death in his bed with a rock – the rock had been left on the scene – but only his cellphone had been stolen. The violence of the attack, so out of proportion to what had been taken, became a hallmark of what came to be known as 'tik murders': violent crimes perpetrated by men high on crystal meth, 'tikkops' who just wanted easy-to-carry merchandise (cellphones and laptops were favourites) to sell quickly on the street for just enough money for their next fix.

Tik, which is usually smoked, is this generation's mandrax: cheap, easy to get hold of and potently addictive, it gives users a feeling of utter invincibility and, often, near-superhuman strength. Cupido thinks about a recent case, when the householder woke up to find a tikkop in his bedroom, and in the ensuing fight the intruder bit a large chunk out of the much bigger and stronger man's arm. The injured man later said about the tikkop (who escaped through a window and was never caught), 'It was amazing: he was so thin and scrawny, about the size of a 12-year-old boy, but he had the strength of ten men.'

Tik use, especially in poorer communities, has become epidemic. One of the detective's younger brothers, Faizel, has fallen victim to this scourge: he dropped out of school because of it, and now in his early 20s he spends his time chasing his next high. Almost everything of any value the Cupido family owns has been taken and sold by Faizel, who's also physically threatened both of their elderly parents, as well as Cupido herself. Although Faizel is seldom at home any more, the family lives in trepidation of when he might turn up next, invariably when he's on the search for money for his next fix.

Skeletal and filthy, mad-eyed and unremittingly angry, Faizel has become known to the community as a problem, and people avoid him. He has used up all the social favours anyone is ever going to extend to him, and Cupido knows it's only a matter of time before he seriously oversteps the mark: it's only a question of how serious his crime will be, and how long he'll be sentenced for.

Her other brother, Zain – the family's youngest child – has, miraculously, managed to escape, not only the tik trap but also the grinding poverty of the lower echelons in the small town, where jobs are few and opportunities fewer. This is thanks in large part to Captain Cupido's own self-sacrifice and commitment to Zain's education and wellbeing. She pays the fees for his attendance at a film school in the city. He's halfway through his second year. She also pays the rent on a tiny room in an overcrowded house in a crappy suburb on the city's outskirts; but it's still better than the hopeless alternative here in the town.

Along with the drastic rise in the use of tik has come a concomitant rise in the numbers of tik murders. One of them, at least, hasn't caused Cupido any lost sleep: the paedophile Allan Knotwood, who for years had evaded jail, had been beaten so savagely about the head and face that it had been nearly impossible to identify him. Were it not for an appendectomy scar and a distinctive tattoo of a clown (oh, the irony) on his lower calf, there might have been doubt as to who'd died in the attack.

Knotwood's business had, by the time of his murder a couple of years ago, collapsed, and his wife had died following a catastrophic stroke. He had lost his house and was living in a back room behind the town's service station. He no longer had a vehicle. His guilt in thirteen cases of child rape was, despite never having been found so in a court of law, undoubted: as his life unravelled, Knotwood had taken to hanging around the town bars late at night, drunkenly telling anyone who would listen that the sex between him and little girls as young as 8 years old had been consensual, that they'd 'asked for it'.

Cupido isn't even sure that Knotwood's death was a tik murder, although officially that's how it's regarded because his cellphone was stolen during the attack. The fatal beating could easily have been perpetrated by someone related in some way to one of the thirteen girls Knotwood had defiled and whose already fragile lives he had ruined. Cupido shrugs to herself: they would probably never know, because as long as she's in charge of this station, not one single second of manpower would be expended in the search for Knotwood's killer.

Cupido can't say she's entirely against a community taking matters into its own hands in certain cases. If she publicly expressed this opinion, she would certainly be fired, but that doesn't stop her thinking it. She muses on the recent case of the theft of a bakkie-load of plants from the nursery out on the national road north of the town. She'd heard about it from Lionel Diez, who'd left the employ of the police a couple of years ago and gone into private security, where he had done very well for himself, with a small team of dedicated men and two highly trained alsations. Diez kept Cupido in the loop on cases he thought she should know about, the nursery theft having been one.

The nursery had gone through some very hard times. The upgrading of the national road had dealt it a body blow, as the entrance, which had been directly off the road, had first been closed for several weeks to enable the building of an alternative route to the nursery, then rerouted via a side road, the turnoff to which wasn't anywhere near the nursery itself, and which was poorly signposted and thus easily missed by most drivers. And the drought had piled on the stress and strain – only the most profligate, or ignorant, of people would have considered new plantings or anything other than the most basic garden maintenance during an extended season of close-to-zero rainfall and insanely high maximum temperatures day after day for months on end.

When the theft of the plants – about thirty, mainly succulents, of different maturities, each lovingly bedded in a beautiful terracotta pot, of several different sizes from medium to very large – had been discovered, the two men who owned the struggling business had needed to do no more than check their security-camera footage to establish the identity of the culprit. Even though the footage was somewhat grainy, both his car's registration and his face were clearly visible – either he hadn't realised he was on camera, or he hadn't cared.

The nurserymen had paid a visit to Harold Backhausen, who lived in the nicer part of the town, in a large house surrounded by an exceptionally well-maintained garden. It became immediately apparent that Backhausen, whose water was supplied solely by the municipality, and who relied on no other recycled or harvested water source to keep his vast lawn green and springy, was one of those most wasteful of people. The nursery's pot plants were still closely and neatly packed in his late-model double-cab bakkie, into which Backhausen had taken his own sweet time loading them the previous night. He'd even helped himself to and used the nursery's hand truck and pot lifter to get the bigger ones into the bakkie.

The reason for the theft was a mystery – this was clearly not a man who needed to sell a haul of pot plants to keep the wolf from the door – and Backhausen had never bothered to enlighten the nurserymen as to his motive. They explained to him that they had evidence of his crime on film, and were on their way to the police station to lay a charge of theft.

'How much to make this go away?' Backhausen had asked them, casually. He'd seemed altogether unembarrassed by his behaviour, and completely unconcerned about having been caught.

'You replace all the pot plants where you found them, immediately, and you donate R10 000 to a charity of our choice,' one of the nurserymen had said.

Backhausen had, incredibly, stood stroking his chin, looking thoughtful. 'That's a lot of money,' he'd said.

The nurserymen had glanced at each other, then one had shrugged his shoulders and said, 'Fine. Have it your way. The next you'll hear about this is from the police.'

Finally, Backhausen had appeared affected. 'Hang on,' he'd said. 'I didn't say I *wouldn't* pay. It's just a lot for …' He'd waved a hand towards the bakkie-load of pot plants.

'It's what those pot plants are worth to us when we sell them to legitimate customers,' the nurseryman had said, earning a disbelieving raised eyebrow from Backhausen, who was apparently rather surprised at how expensive a bakkie-load of pot plants could be.

According to Diez, Backhausen had indeed returned the pot plants, and the nurserymen and their few remaining staff had stood back and watched him unload each and every one alone, the same way he'd loaded them up, intervening only when he placed them in the wrong position, and then only verbally. Not a finger was lifted to help him. 'And it was fokken hot enough to fry an egg on the bonnet of that million-buck bakkie,' Diez had told Cupido, laughing.

The donation had been paid over, too, that same day, to a local animal-welfare charity – the nurserymen were both passionate about dogs. Backhausen, with delicious irony, wasn't that keen on animals, and hated dogs.

Returning her attention to the Imelda Uys case, Cupido briefly entertains the thought that the missing woman may have been attacked and killed by a tikkop for the money in her wallet or the cellphone in her bag, but the officer quickly rejects it. Aside from anything else, tikkops certainly don't go to any trouble to hide or otherwise disguise their victims' bodies.

Taking another sip of the crappy coffee, Sergeant Cupido turns her thoughts to the Bronson/Hallett incident. When the car emerged from the river a couple of days ago, it was reported to the city police, not to her, and they'd taken over the case. Cupido hadn't argued about jurisdiction; in this job, where every bloody pencil and Post-it was hard won, it was wise to pick her battles.

They had arrived yesterday to pick up the case files. It had taken the new admin clerk some time to find the relevant box in the so-called filing cupboard – their filing system for cold cases, a legacy of the old admin clerk, is haphazard, to say the least. So Cupido hadn't had the opportunity to read through the various reports and witness statements to refamiliarise herself with the case, but she remembers most of its details.

The girls had disappeared in the winter of 2010, when record rains fell. The river had burst its banks in lots of places. Things had got washed away. It doesn't surprise her that one of these was the Ford Fiesta that the girls were driving.

It doesn't surprise her either that it was the body of Rosanne Bronson, the learner driver, and not Jess Hallett, the 'responsible' and licensed one, who was found in the driver's seat of the car. The two mothers – Terry and Nicky, she recalls – were both unshakable in their belief that the evidently more sensible girl, Jess, had been driving, because that is what the girl had assured them would be the case. Even the apparently most perfect teenagers lie, Cupido thought. She remembers what kind of teenager she'd been – not dissimilar to Rosanne Bronson – and presses her lips together in cynical recognition.

Cupido thinks about when she went out to the farm to question the Chapels – father and son – and spotted the nicked Alfa Romeo Spider there. She smiles to herself, thinking about the big drugs bust and the dismantling of the stolen car and car-parts ring that had followed – she'd got some grudging praise from the higher-ups for that. It was probably part of the reason for her promotion the next year to captain – not that being captain of this small, undersupplied, overburdened and little-acknowledged branch of the national police force was saying much.

The detective suddenly remembers another detail of that day – the Saturday that she'd driven out to the farm. It had been raining heavily for weeks before, and particularly heavily earlier that morning, and the roads were scattered with debris – tree branches, mainly. But on the bridge she'd spotted a possible serious hazard to drivers: a very large concrete block, which had probably at one time been part of a temporary crash barrier, sticking some way into the traffic lane.

She'd pulled over and stopped the van, then walked back along the hard shoulder to see what she could do to get the obstacle out of the way. It was extremely heavy, and it had taken all her strength to shift it out of the lane, out of the way of passing cars. She'd had to get down on her knees on the wet bridge, digging the toes of her boots into the road's surface and bracing herself against the concrete block, then shoving with all her might, once, twice, three times, to shift it – and even then, she'd been able to move it only marginally, just enough so that it didn't stick out into the lane.

She recalls wondering how the concrete block had ended up there, sticking out into oncoming traffic. She remembers thinking that even the high winds and driving rain couldn't possibly have been strong enough to move it into the road – so how had it got there? She has no way of knowing the answer but because she's learnt, in a decade or so on the job, to put absolutely no faith in human nature, she wouldn't put it past some malicious or stupid person to purposefully have shoved that block into the active-traffic lane, perhaps with the evil intent just to see what would happen when a car came along and hit it.

Well, with the Ford Fiesta having been found, and because of *where* it's been found, Cupido suddenly realises that she knows what probably happened. It seems likely that the Bronson girl, an inexperienced and perhaps reckless driver, as so many teenagers are, had been driving too fast, and either, in the dark and rain, hadn't seen that concrete block on the bridge, sticking out into the traffic lane, or had seen it but had been going too fast to avoid it, and had collided with it. It may have been that collision that had flipped the little car over the crash barrier and into the water.

There's no way of knowing, of course, exactly how the girls had died. Had the impact of the collision, and the flipping of the car and its splashing down into the overfull river, killed them? Or had they drowned in the upside-down vehicle as it sank to the river bed in the violently rushing water? All that has been made public are the bare bones of the story, which the police public-relations department has chosen to tell the media; she doesn't even know, for example, if either or both of the girls had been wearing their seatbelts.

As to the identity – and the motive – of the idiot who'd dragged that concrete block into the path of oncoming cars – well, those they would also never know.

'Jissis. People,' she says to herself.

She's thought about it often since she became a cop. Humans, despite millions of years of civilising evolution, and all our culture and achievements, our triumph over land, air and sea on our own planet, explorations into outer space too, and probably other planets in the near future – despite all that, we still have to lock ourselves up at night, when we're at our most vulnerable, sleeping. If we don't, the chances are high that some other human will exercise the violence and avarice that sets us apart from other species, and beat our brains in.

Seriously, what other species has to lock itself away from others of its own kind at night? the detective thinks to herself. Maybe the monkeys or apes or whatever climb into trees to sleep but that's so that they're safe from their natural predators – leopards or other big cats, she supposes.

'Natural predators,' she murmurs to herself, nodding, appreciating the phrase – it implies an order to things, a fair state of play, a world devoid of unexpected shocks.

Then she shakes her head. When it comes to humans, it's unnatural predators only. People who'll murder you for a cellphone.

Cupido drains her cup and pulls a face. And for all our brilliance, we humans still haven't managed to come up with a half-decent half-affordable coffee either, she thinks.

She sighs and lightly massages her temples with the thumb and middle finger of her left hand. She doesn't know what happened to Nicky Hallett, but she knows that Terry Bronson still lives in the town. She must go and see her, she thinks, as a courtesy, and to offer her condolences.

And, the detective muses, would Mrs Bronson want to know about the concrete block, and her theory about the car colliding with it probably being the cause of how the girls ended up in the river?

Cupido hadn't filed a report about the obstruction at the time.

Having moved it out of the traffic lane, and with no evidence that it had caused any problem for any road user, she'd simply forgotten about it; and it had long since disappeared, either scavenged for use elsewhere, or removed by a road-maintenance crew.

Terry Bronson is going to have a large emotional load to deal with, having to accept that her daughter was the person at the wheel of the car that had become the watery tomb of the two teenagers. Would knowing how the accident may have happened help in any way?

The bodies of the two girls, submerged for six years and probably predated on over time by a variety of aquatic creatures, from large to minuscule, would almost certainly be entirely skeletonised by now. Cupido assumes that post-mortems will be done, and wonders if any signs of foul play will be found on the remains. She doubts it. But she doesn't know for sure.

She decides to keep her theory to herself.

Thursday 25 February
7.02 a.m.

It starts with a single *clck-bzz*, and soon the copse of trees is alive with sound: two hundred and thirteen sun-loving male cicadas, simultaneously vibrating the drum-like tymbals covering the hollow chambers on their abdomen, calling for mates.

In the short adult phase of its life, just one of these thumb-sized winged insects can make a noise that rivals that of a power saw. By the time the sun has cleared the horizon and the heat of the day is setting in, the shrill buzzing is so loud that it sounds like it comes from everywhere at once.

This massed-choir approach serves two purposes: it advertises far and wide that the males are ready and willing to mate; and, equally usefully, the loud noise both repels and confuses birds, making it less likely that too many of these insects will be snatched up and gobbled down in the short time they live above ground.

In the several weeks during which they live in trees, cicadas mate and the females lay eggs. Here, in this copse of eucalyptus, some of them have already done this, carving a groove into a twig with their ovipositor, and laying a single tiny oval egg in it.

The newly hatched young, which look more like little white ants than their big-eyed parents, initially stay in the safety of the groove, feeding on tree fluids. When they're ready to move on to the next stage of their life cycle, they drop to the ground, where they dig themselves in with their shovel-like front legs.

And that's where they stay, sometimes for years. Underground, in tunnels and burrows, they live on roots, growing, shedding their skin at intervals, waiting in solitary darkness for the ideal environmental circumstances and temperature. And when they finally do emerge, it can be in their hundreds or even thousands.

Then, the nymphs will climb the nearest tree, shed their last skin, and enter the world as thumb-sized, big-eyed adults.

Finally, the season of sex has arrived, and the cycle starts all over again.

This is what's happening in the copse of eighteen bluegum trees where the little blue car is cradled, upside down, in its hammock of branches. It's the immutable cycle of being. Beginnings and endings and beginnings; life and death, life and death, and life again.

Inside the blue car, upside down in the driver's seat, the body appears to be reaching its end. It has been absolutely still for many, many hours. But it isn't dead.

Not yet.

Thursday 25 February
9.27 a.m.

Dewald stops his bakkie in the gateway and leans out of the driver's-side window, opening the postbox and pulling out a couple of envelopes and a whole bunch of flyers. Imelda usually brings in the mail, so this lot dates back to Monday.

Vumba is relatively pleased to see him, and lollops out to sniff at the wheels of the bakkie. If she's missing her co-owner, she shows no sign of it.

The heat is already uncomfortable, and Dewald leaves the front door open, then walks through the small house to open the back door, too, chucking the pile of post on the little table of the breakfast nook as he goes by. There's no breeze but it just feels marginally cooler, somehow, with both doors open. Very soon – within an hour or so – he'll have to close up everything, and draw all the curtains, to try to keep as much of the punishing day's heat out of the house as possible.

He runs himself a glass of water from the tap – it comes out hot but he's too aware of the water restrictions to let it run until it's cool – and stands with his back to the sink to drink it. Taking a sip of the unpleasantly warm liquid, he leans forward and rifles with one hand through the mail. The third item down is a flyer from the municipality, with plans for a certain section of the roadworks over the next month: 24-hour stop-go systems, diversions, alternative routes. There'll be no direct access off the national road, from either direction, to Bloekom Farm from the evening of Monday 22 February, he reads, and residents and labourers will have to use the slip road off the—

Dewald puts the glass down on the side of the sink and pushes himself forward. He snatches up and examines the flyer. Monday 22 February: the night Mel disappeared.

Dewald has no idea of the technicalities involved in closing one road and opening an alternative, but he knows that there have to be a few last cars travelling the road before it's closed. And what if Imelda's little blue CitiGolf had been one of those cars? If so, and she'd gone off the old road, not the new road, then he and Detective Cupido have been looking in the wrong places.

Dewald tries to think exactly where the Bloekom Farm turnoff is on the national road. It's a familiar name to him, and he can clearly picture the farm's signboard in his mind's eye – he's driven past it hundreds of times over the years, on trips between home and the town – but, frustratingly, he can't place it precisely.

Grabbing his keys, Dewald rushes out the house, not bothering to close any doors behind him. Vumba, looking mildly interested in this sudden activity, is happy enough to jump into the bakkie, clambering long-legged over the driver's seat to make herself comfortable on the passenger side. Dewald gets in and reverses wildly out of the gravel driveway, the vehicle's wheels kicking up stones.

At the stop street onto the national road that links the little rural community of houses to the town, Dewald turns right. He drives for about fifteen kilometres and then, after a dog-leg he hadn't properly registered before – there are so many of them on this ever-changing road – he hits a section of new road, which he thinks is the one that's only been open for use since Monday night. To be sure, he needs to find Bloekom Farm – but in his memory he holds only the farm's signpost, no other landmarks, and if the signpost has been removed as part of the roadworks, how is he going to recognise what was once the turnoff?

He notes that all the tarmac of the old road, about ten metres to his left, running parallel with the new road, has been chopped up and is lying in piles. He only has to scan the areas on the left side of the road – if Imelda had gone off that old road, and not this new road that he's travelling on, her car will be on that side, off the old road.

A car races up behind him. It's a little hatchback, a young man in the driver's seat, hooting and flashing his lights to try to bully Dewald into going faster. Dewald ignores him, keeping his speed slow and the steady, and continues scanning the roadside. The impatient driver overtakes on one of the sections of road where embankments have been built up – it's a blind rise and Dewald slows down and winces as an oncoming car, hooter blaring, narrowly misses the moron in the hatchback.

Another vehicle takes the place of the hatchback behind him but this driver is less erratic, and slows down to match Dewald's forty-kilometres-an-hour speed, and keeps a reasonable distance between them. Small mercies.

Dewald continues his slow drive and careful scan, but he sees no sign, and eventually the section of new road ends, another dog-leg taking him back onto the old road. Approaching the town, he realises there's nowhere safe to pull off, so he's forced to drive into the town, then make a U-turn and drive out again.

Now he's repeating the exercise the other way – the way Imelda would have been driving back from work, so this is probably a good thing, he thinks. He has another couple of jackasses tailgating him and overtaking dangerously, and he has to dodge one coming towards him, but he determinedly keeps his speed down and keeps searching along the right-hand side. Intermittently, he can see the chopped-up old road running parallel to the new one.

About ten kilometres from the town, with the car behind him hooting furiously, he quickly indicates and stops his bakkie on the roadside. He's realised that the newly built embankments along this stretch of new road are blocking his view to the right, and that any one of them could have prevented him from seeing the Bloekom Farm sign.

He's going to have to walk it.

Thursday 25 February
12.03 p.m.

The small figure walking alongside the jagged, chopped-up surface of the old road shimmers in the heat – mirage-like, it sometimes appears as if it isn't moving at all, and in the next moment it's jumped several metres.

The figure – a man, if its long, loose strides are anything to go by – has his right hand up, shielding his eyes from the battering rays of the midsummer sun. A large wolf-like dog is following close at his heels.

Occasionally the man stops and slowly turns 180 degrees. When he does this, the dog sits and waits.

Clearly, the man is looking for something.

Once, a labourer up the incline on the roadworks shouts something down to the man. The man stops and shouts back. The labourer shakes his head. The seeker moves on, the dog following faithfully.

He walks about two kilometres, his head constantly moving, scanning the right-hand side of the old road, occasionally stopping to do a half-circle search. The dog walks and sits, walks and sits. From time to time it trots ahead.

A short distance from where a team of four labourers are preparing the verges of the new road for installing the huge concrete stormwater channels, the man stops, looks back at where he's come from, then looks ahead again. The dog lopes ahead a few metres, looks back too, sits, tilts its head upwards. Then it stands suddenly, its long tail wagging, and barks – once, twice.

The man questions the dog. The dog barks again. The communication between the man and the dog is unmistakable – the man's entire body shape, curved over, enquiring, is a question; the dog's, its torso rigid, its tail up and both ears erect, is an answer.

The man then looks around slowly, doing another 180-degree turn, and appears to see something that interests him. He lets out a shout and the dog sets off at a run. The man follows.

Man and dog are heading for a copse of eucalyptus trees, alive with cicadas. The sound of the insects carries far and wide, the shrill noise adding intensity to the superheated day.

The duo draw parallel to the copse, then turn and run down the incline, the man quick-stepping, the dog leaping over obstacles. They disappear into the trees.

Above, on the side of the new road, the four workmen have stopped to watch what's happening down below, hands up to shield their faces from the sun.

Neither man nor dog re-emerges for some minutes, and the labourers lose interest. Two of them return to the task at hand, and the other two are about to follow suit when they hear a shout from below.

The man comes barrelling out of the stand of trees. '*Help!*' he screams. '*Get help!*'

Monday, 28 February 2016 – A woman who spent three days trapped upside down in a wrecked vehicle in temperatures that reached over 40 degrees has severe injuries, but her brain function is normal, according to her doctors.

Imelda Uys, 29, was found alive but severely dehydrated in a stand of eucalyptus trees at the bottom of an incline off the national road, three days after she failed to return home from work. After being cut out of her car by emergency rescuers, she was taken to a nearby hospital, where she was admitted in critical condition. She is sedated, on a ventilator and being treated with intravenous fluids.

A spokesperson for the hospital said, 'Her kidneys failed because of toxins from injuries she got in the crash and from dehydration.' Uys broke her right collarbone and dislocated her right shoulder, and broke bones in her right arm and hand. Both her legs were crushed, and she may have spinal injuries. 'She's probably only alive because she's young and healthy, and because she was wearing her seatbelt,' the spokesperson said.

No other car was involved in the incident. It is thought that Uys, who holds down two jobs, fell asleep at the wheel while on her way home late on Monday afternoon. Her car left the road and crashed into the stand of trees, where the impact caused it to flip. That section of road was closed the same evening, as part of an ongoing road-upgrade project.

Denver Sully, a foreman on the roadworks, said that that stretch of the road was usually busy, and that it was just bad luck that nobody had seen Uys's car leave the road. 'Once the car had gone into the trees, there was no sign of it,' he said. 'I sat against one of the trees and ate my lunch one day last week, and I had no idea it was there.'

Acknowledgements

Thank you to my first reader and cheerleader Lynda du Plessis, my second reader Lynn McNamara for her informed and useful feedback, and my sister Beverley Hawthorne for her constant encouragement.

Thank you to my father, Peter Hawthorne, who instilled in me a love of story-telling and set the example, and the colleagues who have inspired me and encouraged my writing, especially Hilary Prendini Toffoli, Jane Raphaely, Daniel Ford, Gill Cullinan and Karin Schimke.

Thanks to Tanya Majo for her clever cover concept and beautiful artworks, and Santa van der Walt for her cover design.

Thanks to Dr Brian Manning for checking the medical info and to David Bristow for checking environmental and other information – any errors are mine.

Thanks to publisher Colleen Higgs and Modjaji Books, to editor Fiona Zerbst for her incisive and creative input, and to Jane-Anne Hobbs for her meticulous proofreading.

Finally, thanks to my family, Daniel, Isabella, Joel and Jessie, for always keeping it both real and funny.

Printed in the United States
by Baker & Taylor Publisher Services